A Grump in MOOSE FALLS

Cover Design by Seaj Art

Editing by Happily Editing Anns

www.authoremilysilver.com

A GRUMP IN MOOSE FALLS

A Moose Falls Series Novella

EMILY SILVER

To every reader this holiday season…
Sending you lots of joy and love
<3

Chapter One

OLLIE

A SOUP SIZED DISASTER

"**I** can't wait to meet your boyfriend."

The shrill voice startles me, my spoon clattering to the desk. Tomato bisque splatters across the neatly printed stack of papers.

"What are you talking about, Sharon?" I ask, grabbing a napkin to mop up the mess.

"The company Christmas party this weekend. All of our significant others were invited this year."

"W-what?" I stutter.

"Did you read Kevin's email?"

"No. I'm eating my soup."

She sighs. "You really should eat your lunch in the break room."

"I like eating at my desk."

The likelihood of having to socialize is much lower here, which gives me less of a chance of being awkward.

"What did this email say?" I ask, ignoring her.

"Details of the party. When and where. And *who* is invited, more importantly."

"I thought significant others couldn't come since Terry's partner got drunk and tore the paper towel dispenser off the wall at the bar."

"Kevin decided to give them a second chance."

"He did?" I adjust my glasses.

"Which means"—she beams at me—"we get to meet this elusive boyfriend of yours."

"I'm going to have to run it by him."

"No one's worried about you bringing a man. Kevin and Raymond have been married for years," Sharon points out, like that's the hang-up.

"I'm not worried. He is busy this time of year, so I need to check his schedule."

Sharon pierces me with a sharp look. Being older and having two kids and several grandkids, I'm sure it's the look she uses to get them to tell her the truth if they're lying.

I squirm under the attention.

"You're not getting out of it, so make sure you bring him so we can all meet him. Since you've been talking about him so much, it's about time you bring him around."

"Right." I grimace.

Bangles clang as she walks away, leaving me to myself. I groan, dropping my head onto my desk.

My still messy, soup-stained desk.

Crap. I can feel half-dried soup sticking to my forehead.

This is not how I was planning on spending my day. Working on the latest specs for a new library remodel? Yes.

Taking a boyfriend that doesn't exist to a company Christmas party?

No.

Everyone here is in everyone's business all the time. If I

didn't like my job so much, I might leave. But architect jobs are hard to find in small-town Maine. Even this job isn't in Moose Falls.

I could only fend off Sharon and her wanting to set me up with her cousin's boyfriend's best friend's brother so many times before I snapped.

I'm not the type that likes to go out after work, so I didn't see any harm in saying I had someone at home. They let it go.

It's going to be even worse if I show up and I don't have anyone. Crap. Well, maybe… I mean, this is why they have dating apps, right? Except the thought of getting on a dating app petrifies me.

I can't show up dateless. There's only a handful of people who would understand.

OLLIE

Mayday! Mayday!

HUNTER

What's the emergency?

Why do you assume there's an emergency?

HUNTER

You texted mayday

HUNTER

That is the universal sign for distress

I don't know if it's an emergency…

GRIFFIN

What's wrong?

I need your help

Something's come up at work

GRIFFIN

Just name the time and place

GRIFFIN

We'll be there

GRIFFIN

If Theo can peel himself away from his new boyfriend

THEO

Hey, don't hate on me because I'm in love

CHARLIE

I'll reserve the usual spot for us

BROOKS

And I'll already be there since Charlie will be there

I BLOW out a breath as I mop up the rest of my soup with a napkin from my desk. I'll have to reprint everything I was working on. Notes made. Numbers calculated. At least it'll be easy enough to redo.

Why can't I be cool and keep my composure?

Maybe if I were, I wouldn't be in this situation. An awkward, bumbling nerd who is hopelessly single. Not that I mind most days.

I like my life. I love getting to design buildings for a living. I have a close group of friends who are like family, since my own family lives across the country.

So what if I don't date? So what if I've never had sex? It's not like my life depends on those two things.

Then why am I starting to sweat?

Heading to the bathroom to clean up, I set my glasses on the counter and splash cold water on my face.

Staring at myself in the mirror, I give myself a mental pep talk. I can do this. It's one night. One night isn't a big deal.

I can figure something out for one night. I've solved a lot harder problems at work. But I'll find something temporary. I have to. Because I don't want my coworkers to know I've been lying. That'd be even worse.

Solving the problem of Ollie needing a boyfriend? Not sure that one will ever be solved.

Chapter Two

HUNTER

AN AX TO GRIND

"Which tree do you want?"

"Aren't they all the same?" the little boy with a wide-toothed smile asks.

"They aren't." I kneel down next to him and point to two different trees. "That one is taller, and that one right there has more needles. Very different."

"They look the same to me."

"Well, whichever one you want, you'll need to make sure it fits in your house. You wouldn't want to cut your tree in half."

He shakes his head, pointing to the fuller tree. "I want that one then."

His mom smiles and nods behind him.

"Then stand back."

Making sure the area is clear, I line up my trusty ax and take a mighty swing.

Thwack.

It cracks right into the trunk of the tree at a perfect

angle. The vibrations ripple through my arms as I cut into it before it falls to the ground with a soft thud.

"Wow! I want to learn to do that!"

"Maybe when you're older." I smile at him before directing my attention to his mom. "We'll get this taken out to your car and tied down for you."

"Great."

"There's some hot cocoa at the main barn or a train if you want to ride through the fields."

"Can we, Mom? Please?" the little boy asks, pulling on her coat sleeve.

"Let's go."

They wave at me as they head off into the snow-covered rows of trees toward the main barn of Naughty Pine Tree Farm.

I whistle as I make quick work of pulling the Scotch pine tree onto the sled to get wrapped in netting.

It's just the distraction I need to keep from worrying about Ollie and whatever problem he might have. Normally he would have texted me by now to tell me what it is. Seeing as how he's my best friend—and I'm his—he'll usually tell me before the other guys.

Does that means something could really be wrong? No. He wouldn't have texted that. He would have called.

God love my best friend, but he is still someone that prefers a phone call over texting. It's only because it's him that I take his call. Checking my phone one more time, I see nothing.

At least I can head to the Tinsel Tavern once I'm done with this tree. Perks of being the owner. I can play hooky when I need to.

Not that I make a habit of doing it, but a few hours in the middle of busy season is about all I can manage.

For Ollie? I'd give him the whole day if needed.

By the time I finish up, I'm running a few minutes behind as I hop into my truck and head into town.

I blast one of my favorite Christmas songs—"All I Want For Christmas Is You"— because who doesn't love it? I don't go around advertising that. I have to keep up my grumpy lumberjack façade with my friends.

The Tinsel Tavern is packed. Circling the block a few times, it takes me a while to find a parking spot. As I'm getting out, my phone buzzes in my pocket.

MOM

Cindy has a single son

Any interest?

HUNTER

Are we back on this again?

I know you said you weren't dating, but he's handsome

I told you

I'm fine on my own

Please

It's okay to admit you want someone

I'm in no rush to settle down

Fine

Pass up this handsome man

I'll die alone with no son-in-law

Bye, Mom

SHAKING MY HEAD, I stuff my phone into my jeans pocket and head inside. Of course my mom is trying to set me up. It's the last thing I want. I love my life exactly how it is.

After moving away from Moose Falls after college with my boyfriend, I thought I had everything figured out. Life was good. I thought the two of us were going to get married. I was head over heels in love until the rug was pulled out from under me. Turns out, I wasn't the only one he was in love with.

Whenever it comes to relationships? I turn into a bear.

The thought of them makes me do a complete one-eighty. My mom trying to hook me up? I can't help being standoffish.

When I moved back here, I swore off relationships.

Trees? I like my trees. And my friends.

Relationships?

I don't do them. I like playing the field. It's fun. There's nothing wrong with casual sex. It works for me.

Something I don't really tell my mom, so I go with reminding her I'm not ready to settle down.

Besides, my schedule is chaotic at best during the holidays. I don't want to have someone waiting on me when I won't be home until all hours of the night.

"Look who finally decided to show up," Brooks says, fingers balancing three drinks as he weaves his way through the crowd when I step inside.

"Some of us had to work today."

"If I could flip you off, I would."

I grin back at him. "I know."

"Forgot all the hard work I did for *you* today."

My grin gets bigger. "While I've been chopping down trees."

"Because you won't let me near the ax."

"For good reason."

I love Brooks, mainly because it's so easy to give him shit. He's been good for Charlie this last year, and I've loved seeing the two of them grow together as a couple.

Not something I want anymore because I'm perfectly happy on my own, but they seem to be doing just fine.

"What's this big emergency?" I ask, grabbing a beer from Brooks and sliding into the round booth at the back of the bar with Griffin, Theo, and Ollie. Christmas lights are twinkling as holiday songs play from the jukebox.

"Technically, I was not the one that called it an emergency," Ollie clarifies, adjusting his glasses. Having known him my entire life—our mothers met in the hospital and became best friends—I know this is his nervous tic.

"I, well…" he starts and stops.

I sip on my drink, letting him take all the time he needs to gather his thoughts. I grab a pretzel from the bowl Charlie brought over and pop it into my mouth.

"You're worrying me," Griffin says.

"I need a boyfriend."

Coughing, my pretzel gets lodged in my throat. Charlie pats me on the back as I swig down my drink to try and clear it.

"I'm sorry, what? A boyfriend?"

"Yes." His cheeks turn cherry red.

I don't think I've ever seen him turn this color before.

"Why do you need a boyfriend?" Theo asks.

"It's a long story."

"We have plenty of time." Griffin rests his arm on the back of the booth, looking at him.

Ollie picks at his beer bottle. "I kind of told my coworkers I was dating someone."

"You kind of told them or you *did* tell them?" Brooks asks. "Just for clarification here."

"I told them I was dating someone." Ollie sighs, then gulps down a large swig of beer and nearly chokes on it.

"You need a boyfriend," Charlie reiterates. "What for?"

"The company Christmas party is this Friday and significant others are invited."

"I thought they were banned?" I question. "Didn't someone get drunk and start a fire?"

"Someone started a fire?" Theo asks. "I don't know if I've heard that story."

"No, there was no fire," Ollie interjects. "Someone got drunk and thought it would be a good idea to rip a paper towel dispenser off the wall."

"Why'd you tell them you were dating someone if you're not? I mean, it seems pretty easy to just say you're single," Griffin adds.

"They wouldn't stop pestering me about dating someone, so one day I snapped and told them I was seeing someone so they'd drop it."

"Ahh." I nod my head. That sounds about right. "With the party coming up, you need to take someone so it doesn't look like you were lying."

"Correct."

"Could you try a dating app?" Theo asks. "I mean, Trey and I met that way."

Griffin snorts. "I still can't believe you're dating someone named Trey."

"At least I'm dating someone." Theo throws a knowing look toward his best friend.

"Ouch. Tell me how you really feel."

"I'm only saying you could meet someone if you wanted to."

Griffin shakes his head. "I'm fine playing the field."

"I don't think that's what Ollie wants to do, right?" I

ask, interrupting the two of them before they really get going.

"N-no," he mutters. "I don't think that would give us enough time to get to know one another to make it believable that we're in a relationship together. Besides, what would I say? 'Wanted—one fake boyfriend for the holiday to fake out his coworkers'?"

"You need someone who knows you," Charlie says, tapping his chin. "Why don't you take one of those guys?"

He points to the three of us sitting next to him.

"Don't look at me," Theo says. "I am happy in my relationship and don't want to explain to Trey why I'm going on a date with someone else."

"*Fake* date," Ollie corrects. "It would only be one night."

"Which leaves one of you two," Brooks says, looking between Griffin and me.

"I think I'm free Friday," Griffin states.

"You are?" Ollie swings his gaze to him, studying him. Like he's seriously considering taking this man to his holiday party.

Which leads me to what I say next.

"I'll do it."

Every set of eyes bores into me.

"You will?"

"I just offered," Griffin says. "What's wrong with me?"

"Nothing. I'm free. I'll do it," I repeat.

"Apparently I'm chopped liver," Griffin says to Theo.

"I still love you." Theo pecks him on the cheek.

"You'd really do it?" Ollie asks. "I feel bad for even asking. I don't want to make you uncomfortable."

I give him an easy smile. "It's not a big deal. Besides, if there's someone that is going to be a good fake boyfriend, it's going to be me. I know you better than I know myself some days."

"This is true," Griffin states, like it's a balm to him not being picked.

"It's only for one night," Ollie points out. "Nothing else."

"It's fine," I say. "I can do one night. Having to hang with my friend? Not the end of the world."

Hell, it'll probably be a better night than I had planned. Working late at the farm then home and a beer before crashing?

Yeah, much better.

Given how busy I am this time of year, it'll be nice to get out for once.

"Why don't you come over tomorrow and we can go over all the details?" Ollie asks, once again adjusting his glasses.

"Sounds good."

I shoot a wink his direction before downing the rest of my beer and heading to the bar to order another round.

"You sure you know what you're doing?" Charlie asks, following behind me to help.

"It's one night. What could possibly happen in one night that will change things?"

"Just making sure," he says.

"Thanks, but we're good."

We're Hunter and Ollie. Nothing is going to change that.

Not even one night as boyfriends.

Fake boyfriends. I can't forget that part.

One night as fake boyfriends won't change anything.

Chapter Three

HUNTER

FOR MY FRIEND

I really don't know what came over me the other night. Saying yes to Ollie's plan to be his fake boyfriend seemed to make the most sense.

I mean, it's not like it's real. I don't have to worry about turning into a madman and taking out my relationship issues on others. It's why I never have a boyfriend. I don't like who I become when I'm dating someone.

See what I mean? I'm a bear.

I'm driving to his place now to work out the finer details of it, and things feel different. I can't pinpoint why. I'm doing this to be a good friend.

Ollie isn't the best at social situations, so being able to help him out is what any friend would do.

So again, why am I nervous?

Knocking on his door, I don't wait for him to answer before walking in.

"Hey, Ollie."

His head pops up from where he's standing in the kitchen. Heat from the stove fogs his glasses as his brown hair flops over his forehead. "Hey. Sorry, I'm almost done."

"Take your time." I toe off my boots, caked with mud from working this morning, and pad my way toward the counter. "What are you making? Smells good."

"Cheeseburger soup. I figured I could feed you as a thank you."

Heading to the fridge, I grab a bottle of the beer Ollie keeps for me. "You don't have to do that."

Ollie reaches to the shaker-style cabinets that I helped him remodel a few years ago and pulls out two bowls. "I know, but I appreciate what you're doing for me."

"I'd do it for any of my friends."

"You would?" he asks, ladling out two big spoonfuls in each bowl.

"Of course."

"That makes me feel better," he says, grabbing a beer and walking over to the dining room table before going back to bring out our soup bowls. "I don't want you taking pity on me."

It's cozy here. After his parents moved out west, we revamped everything in his childhood home. Knocked down some walls so the first floor flowed. Ollie wanted a bigger kitchen since he loves spending so much time in there.

Always on his soups.

"Why would I do this out of pity?" It comes out as more of a growl, but I don't like it when Ollie talks down about himself.

"Hunter, come on. We all know I'm the most awkward person in the entire world. I don't want to be a burden to anyone, especially you. And you hate relationships."

I shake my head, grabbing the pepper shaker from the

table and adding some to my bowl. "You know you're not a burden to me. You're my best friend."

"I wish we didn't have to do this." Ollie stirs his soup around, not looking at me. "Maybe if I let them set me up, we wouldn't be in this situation."

A possessive feeling washes through me. Why does the thought of Ollie being set up by his coworkers make me feel like this? It's not like *we're* dating.

"You could tell them we broke up and have them set you up."

"I don't know if I'm ready for that." His eyes go wide. "They'd be a bit too much about it."

I smile at him, digging into my soup. Delicious, as always. "Then I'll be there for you Friday, and we won't have to worry about it going forward."

Ollie sighs. "Okay. What's our story going to be?"

"Our story?"

"You know, how we met?"

"Keep it simple and tell the truth." The small chair creaks under my weight as I lean back and kick my feet out. "There's no need to overly complicate things."

"But how did we become more?"

I sip my beer, thinking on it before it dawns on me. "You wooed me with your soups."

He rolls his eyes. "Be serious, Hunter."

I laugh. "I am. What's wrong with that? I could have been sick one day and you brought me chicken noodle soup to nurse me back to health. I've been a goner ever since."

He waggles his head back and forth. "I mean, I guess that could work."

"It will, because anyone that knows you knows how much you love soup. It's your love language."

Ollie blushes. "I mean, I would do it if you really were sick. Minus the falling for me part."

"Who knows?" I shrug a shoulder. "Maybe some guy will be at the bar, see you, come over and talk to you, and the rest will be history?"

He snorts. "Okay, nice try. That won't happen, but at least I feel better about how this whole thing started."

"Any other questions your coworkers are liable to ask?"

"First date. How serious we are. Are we getting married?"

"Shit, really? That seems nosy to me."

He nods, adjusting his glasses. "They like to be involved in everyone's personal lives. Hence why they keep trying to set me up."

"Well, in case they ask…how serious are we?"

His blush grows even darker. This is something that always happens to Ollie. *Always*. No matter what, any time there is a hint of digging into his personal life, this happens. He doesn't like being the center of attention.

"Umm, how about exclusive? Is that okay?"

"Works for me. Most exclusive relationship I've had in a while." I nod. "If they ask, I'll be sure to answer."

He blows out a breath, going back to his soup. "Thank you. You know how nervous I get."

"I know." I reach across the table and squeeze his forearm. A warmth spreads through me. One that is not entirely unwelcome. It's only because I'm helping my friend. "I'll make sure I'm likeable, but not so likeable that they want to invite us out again."

"Seems like a fine line to walk," he says, staring at his arm where I've just pulled my hand away from him.

"Trust me, I'll make sure we get through the night in one piece."

"I might need more drinks than normal."

"Uh-oh." I smile. "Is four-drink Ollie going to come out? Maybe even five?"

He covers his face with his hands. "I don't know what will happen if I have five drinks. I can barely handle the one I have when we go out."

"I will make sure you keep it in check."

"Thanks, Hunter. You're a good friend for doing this with me. I know not everyone wants to be their friend's fake boyfriend, but it means a lot to me."

That same warmth from earlier blooms in my chest. "You know I'm always here for you. No matter what you need."

"Well, if I can ever return the favor, I'd be happy to."

I snort laugh. "If I'm ever in the market for a fake boyfriend to impress Brooks, I'll let you know."

That earns me an easy smile. "You do have more people than just Brooks that work for you."

"He's the only one in the office that would say something. And he knows we don't need to do that."

"Favor still stands. I'll say you brought me soup when I was sick and you won me over."

"Good to know all it takes is soup in this relationship to win us over."

Ollie laughs. "I'm easy."

"Oh you are, are you?" I waggle my brows at him. "Good thing to know about my *boyfriend*."

"W-what? No. I didn't mean it like...th-th-that," he stutters.

"Damn. I was thinking I might get lucky."

"Hunter!" he hisses. "We cannot do...that. It won't be—"

He cuts himself off.

"Won't be what?" Now I'm curious as to what he was going to say.

"I don't want to say." He shakes his head.

"Okay."

"That's it? You're not going to keep pressing?"

I drain the last of my soup. "Nope. If you don't want to tell me, you don't have to."

"Wow. I thought you'd keep asking questions about why I've never had sex."

"Wait, what?"

"Oh, no." He buries his face in his hands. "I can't believe I said that out loud."

"It's okay."

"No, it's not. I don't want people to think I'm weird because I haven't had sex before."

"No one thinks you're weird, Ollie." My tone is firm.

He peeks one greenish-brown eye at me through his fingers. "You don't?"

I shake my head.

"No. You're my best friend. I don't think you're weird at all."

Honestly? I'm not surprised. Ollie has never been the most forward of people. And who cares? If he doesn't want to date, he doesn't need to date. He's happy, and that's all that matters to me.

"It's just, all of you guys talk about dating and finding someone, and that's never exactly been something I'm concerned with."

"You don't have to do anything you don't want to do."

"I know." He drops his hands and his eyes go wide. "You're not going to tell the guys, are you?"

"Fuck, no, Ol. It's not my news to tell. Promise."

"Good."

"Look"—I rest my elbows on the table and lean forward—"you and I are going to go to the party on Friday and have a great time. People will think we're a great couple and it will be because you and I are friends. After? I'll drop you off at home and you won't have to worry about it again. Sound good?"

He nods. "Okay. I can do it."

"Good. Now, finish your soup before it gets cold."

Chapter Four

OLLIE

SURVIVAL

"Do I look okay?" I ask, not for the first time tonight.

"Would you relax?" Hunter smacks my hand away from my tie so I won't keep messing with it. "You look great."

"Really?" I adjust my glasses, looking down at the white shirt with a festive tie and my standard black jacket.

"Promise."

"I worry people are going to take one look at us and realize I'm lying," I confess. "I feel like it's written all over my forehead."

"Hey." Hunter grabs my bicep, pulls me off the sidewalk, and presses me up against the side of the building. "No one is going to know this isn't real unless you blurt it out to them. We'll go in there, have a few drinks, and chat with your coworkers before going home."

"You know I'm prone to blurt things, right?"

He smiles at me. "I know. But if you think you're in danger of saying anything, just say eggplant."

"Eggplant?" I laugh. "Really, Hunter?"

My shoulders release the pent-up tension I've been carrying around since he picked me up earlier tonight.

This close, I can see Hunter's playful brown eyes. A shudder racks my body at how they are fixed solely on me.

Wait, *what?* That's a new feeling. Hunter has looked at me thousands of times, probably hundreds of thousands of times since we grew up together, and it's never elicited *this* kind of response.

I ignore the feeling. It's not what I need to be worried about right now.

"Got you to relax, didn't it? Besides, we're friends. People aren't going to question how well we know each other."

"You haven't met Sharon. She'll want to know everything."

"Then it's a good thing I know everything about you, Ollie. You can quiz me if it makes you feel better."

I pin him with a look that says I want to do this but don't want to say it because I don't want to insult him. Like saying it is going to make it even more apparent that we aren't dating.

"Fine," he says. "You're Ollie. We met when we were babies at the hospital because our moms were best friends. You've had glasses since second grade and you're a superhero movie junkie. Soup is the only food group you care about, and though you won't admit it, you love watching the gardening channel because it calms you down, despite having a black thumb."

I straighten. "Okay, I guess we'll be okay."

"I told you we would."

Hunter winks at me before stepping back onto the sidewalk and heading toward the restaurant. I can't help it—

my nerves are still on edge. Mainly because of how he made me feel.

Sound filters out from the bar. Music. Laughter. The happy chatter of voices. I wish attendance at this holiday party wasn't required. It's probably because people like me would choose to stay home.

Even though I love my job, I don't like being social with people I don't know well. And after all these years, I still consider my coworkers just that—coworkers.

Hunter holds the door open and sweeps his arm out in front of me. "After you."

"Wow. You really know how to play up this whole boyfriend thing."

"It's called being chivalrous." He winks at me.

"It's a wonder you're not already taken," I whisper.

Loud music practically slaps me in the face as we step inside. Our owner rented out the entire place for us tonight. Tables are filled with food, and a line of people waiting for drinks wraps around the bar .

"Want me to get us drinks?" Hunter asks.

"I'll go with you."

Scanning the crowd, I'm not quite ready to be on my own. I don't want anyone thinking I'm here by myself and having to answer *those* questions.

"Ollie! You made it," Sharon's voice rings out.

I jump, running smack-dab into Hunter's chest. He settles a hand on my waist.

"Relax," he whispers into my ear. "Everything is fine."

"Right," I say more to myself than anything.

"I can't believe we're meeting Ollie's boyfriend," Sharon says.

I don't move, still stuck in Hunter's grasp. His hand gives me a possessive squeeze, letting me know I'm okay.

And boy, am I ever okay when Hunter touches me like that.

"Sharon, this is my boyfriend, Hunter. Hunter, this is Sharon."

Tinsel trees hang from her ears as her sweater lights up, flashing various colors at me.

"It is very nice to meet you," she says, sticking her hand out.

Hunter takes it, giving her a smile. "It's nice to finally meet some of Ollie's coworkers."

"I hope you don't take offense I kept trying to set Ollie up. I only want to see him happy."

"Believe me, we're happy."

I turn my head back to look at Hunter, his eyes shining down at me.

Huh.

He really does look happy. Even under that scruffy beard of his, I can see happiness radiating from him.

Hunter really is a good actor.

"I can see that." I turn my attention back to Sharon, and she looks like the cat that got the canary. "I'll let you two grab drinks and get settled. I'll see you around."

With that, she's off. No doubt to tell everyone that she just met Ollie's boyfriend.

"Great. Everyone is going to know we're here in about five minutes."

Hunter laughs. "Five minutes? More like five seconds. She was *giddy* at meeting me."

I smack his chest as we move forward in line. With several bartenders working, the line moves quickly.

"We don't need to inflate your ego."

"Ollie. I heard you made it."

The owner of the firm, Kevin, waltzes up with his

husband on his arm. They are both in tacky Christmas sweaters.

"Hi, Kevin. Raymond." I reach around to loop my arm through Hunter's. "This is my boyfriend, Hunter."

"It's very nice to meet you."

They all shake hands and introduce themselves.

"Thanks for inviting us," Hunter says. "Any night out with this guy is a great evening."

Hunter presses a kiss to the top of my head, sending a fissure of emotions crashing through me. He really is laying it on thick.

"As long as you don't go crazy on the open bar and rip things off of walls." Kevin laughs, but I know he's serious.

Hunter holds up his hands. "I promise. I won't get out of line."

"Good. You two enjoy yourselves."

More people come up and introduce themselves to us, and by the time a bartender waves us forward, my nerves are fried.

"Two shots of cinnamon whisky and two beers," I say.

"Coming right up."

"And whatever he's having." I throw a thumb over my shoulder to Hunter.

"Those aren't for me too?" He quirks a brow at me. "Hitting it pretty hard, aren't you?"

"Yes." I nod. "I need all the liquid courage I can get to make it through this evening."

Two shot glasses are set on the bar, and I suck them down back-to-back. Hunter's eyes go wide.

"Am I going to be picking you up off the floor later?"

"No."

At least I don't think so. But we'll see. I'm already at my limit of socialization and the evening has only just begun.

I hope I can survive it.

Chapter Five

THE BEST BOYFRIEND EVER

"We need more shots!" someone calls out. I'm not sure who. After dinner, the drinks started flowing. I'm guessing with an open bar, people will get their fill.

"Ollie, you want more?"

"Yes," he answers.

"You sure?" I ask Ollie. His eyes are starting to glaze over behind his glasses.

"I'm totally fish."

"Fish?" I laugh.

"Fine. I meant fine." He hiccups.

A tray of shots is brought out and Ollie grabs two, downing both. I don't think I've ever seen him drink this much.

"You're a lot of fun, Sharon," Ollie tells the woman standing next to him. "We should go out more often."

Her eyes light up. Christmas lights from her sweater sparkle in her eyes. "We should. You can bring Hunter. We'll have soooo much fun."

"We can make crackers."

"Crackers?" I question Ollie, sipping on my drink. "What are crackers?"

"Crackers, Hunter. *Crackers*."

"The food?"

"There's a cracker farm. They grow crackers. We can *make* crackers," Sharon says, like it's the most obvious thing in the world.

"Okay, whatever you two want." I sip on my water, shaking my head at these two.

"Kevin!" Ollie shouts.

"Ollie, you rang?"

"We need to go make crackers." He giggles. Straight-up giggles.

"Crackers? Where can we make crackers? This will be the next office party. Excellent idea," Kevin says.

Crackers? Really?

I have no idea where this came from and have no idea what Ollie is even talking about.

"We could even make soup!" Ollie claps his hands, he's so excited at the idea. "Everyone could come over to my house for a soup day."

"What?"

This time, I really am confused. I've never heard Ollie invite anyone over to his house. He only invites the guys over on rare occasions.

Eight-drink Ollie apparently wants to be the center of attention.

"A soup night? I love this idea." Sharon claps, her eyes glowing. "We could do it after cracker day."

"Yes." Ollie hiccups. "We have to do this!"

Ollie sways into me and I wrap a supportive arm around his waist.

"Aww. You two are so sweet together," Sharon coos. "How did you guys start dating?"

"Umm…" Ollie starts.

"I was sick one day and he brought me soup to make me feel better. It was perfect and we've been dating ever since."

"That's so precious."

"What can I say? I know the way to my man's heart," Ollie says, turning his drunken gaze to me.

His eyes are like hot chocolate, warm and soft. The feeling of his gaze slides through me, heating me from the inside out. A shudder racks my body at the way he is studying me.

I want to kiss him.

Shit.

I don't know if we could get away with that. Ollie is a bit too drunk and I don't want to do anything to throw him off his game. He's doing great so far tonight.

Even if he's talking about going to a cracker-making class with his coworkers.

"I wish my husband knew me as well as you two know each other," Sharon says.

"Well, we have known each other all of our lives," I say. "Makes it easy."

"You two really are the cutest. I'm just so happy that Ollie is happy. So happy," Sharon says. If possible, she's more drunk than Ollie.

"I'm soooo happy," Ollie slurs. "Hunter is the best. The best boyfriend ever."

"Why have you kept this slab of man all to yourself?" Sharon asks. "He is quite handsome, Ollie."

"He is *so* handsome," Ollie repeats.

"Okay. I think it's time to head home." I grab the drink

from Ollie and set it on the table. "We don't need to hear how handsome I am."

"But you are," Ollie slurs. "The handsomest boyfriend. To ever handsome."

"Sharon, it was very nice to meet you. I need to get this guy in bed."

"Damn right you do!" she shrieks.

"Not what I meant." I shake my head. Ollie sways, ready to pass out.

Looping my arm around his waist, I steer him out of the bar. A cold gust of wind hits us smack in the face.

"Sharon really likes you. Like, really, really likes you." Ollie hiccups.

"She was nice."

"She thought you were quite handsome too."

"I think you did as well."

"Because you are. I mean, have you seen yourself?"

I smile. "Okay, now I know you're drunk."

"I can be drunk and think you're hot, Hunter." Ollie comes to a dead stop on the sidewalk. "Oh my God. Did I say that out loud?"

"It's fine." I grab his hand and try to drag him to the car, but for a drunk person, he's surprisingly strong.

"I really shouldn't think about your abs. I know you have them. I felt them. And those tree-cutting arms. So strong."

"Do I need to put them to good use tonight and carry you to the car?"

"You would?"

I step in front of him and stare down at him. His breath comes out in puffs in the cold air. "Yes. You, Ollie, are drunk and need to get home. You're going to have a wicked hangover tomorrow."

He slaps at my chest. "I'll be fine."

"Sure."

This time, when I start walking, he comes with me. Opening the passenger door, I help Ollie inside and make sure he gets buckled in. His soft hands try to swat mine away, but hold on instead.

"Thank you, Hunter."

"For what?"

His head is resting on the back of the seat, eyes closed.

"For tonight coming. I mean, coming tonight."

"Hey." I flip my hand over and squeeze his. "You know I'm here for you. Mainly because otherwise you wouldn't get home."

"Right."

The rest of the ride home is quiet, Ollie now snoring next to me. Soft music plays in the cab of my truck as I tap my thumbs on the steering wheel.

Tonight was a fun, but weird, night. When Ollie needed a fake boyfriend, I figured it'd be like any other night when the two of us hang out.

Turns out, it was anything but.

It felt good, way too good, to be on Ollie's arm. To have him stare at me with something like…affection?

It was the alcohol. Definitely. Because Ollie isn't feeling anything for me other than friendship.

I scrub a hand down my face as I pull into his driveway. I need to lock up these feelings for Ollie. He doesn't feel the same. I don't want to jeopardize our friendship. It's a one-night thing.

That's it.

Since he's still half asleep, I help Ollie inside and into his room. He collapses onto his bed immediately. I undo the laces on his shoes and toss them to the side.

"Will you spend the night?" Ollie sighs as he sinks into

his mattress. A happy, drunk smile sits on his face. "Please, Hunter?"

"You got it."

Okay, so maybe a two-day thing.

Then that's it.

For real.

Chapter Six

HUNTER

BACK INTO A PUMPKIN

Shouldering open the front door, I balance the coffee, bagels, and plastic bag dangling from my fingers.

"Hunter? Is that you?"

A groan echoes from deep inside Ollie's house.

"It's me."

Toeing off my boots and shaking the snow from my coat, I drop everything onto the counter, grab the one thing I need, and find Ollie slumped over his toilet.

"How you feeling there, champ?"

"Ugh. Why did you let me drink so much?"

"I tried stopping you, but you're the one that decided to keep going."

He peers up at me, one eye open, sweat clinging to his forehead. "Isn't that your job as my boyfriend?"

"Technically, I'm no longer your boyfriend. And I did try to stop you."

"Why didn't I let you?" he groans.

"Because you were the life of the party. Talking about making crackers."

"Oh, God, really? Ugh. Remind me never to drink that much again."

I unscrew the cap of the bottle I'm holding and hand it over to him. "Drink this. It'll make you feel better."

He shakes his head, closing his mouth. "I don't know if I'm going to be able to stomach that."

"I got the blandest flavor I could. Electrolytes help everyone."

"I usually make myself soup and then curl up on the couch and watch movies all day."

"Well, then,"—I grab a washcloth from the cabinet and wet it down—"if you can pull yourself together, I'll order us some soup and we can watch some Christmas movies on the couch together."

"Is this part of your boyfriendly duties?" he asks, eyes closing as I press the cool cloth to his forehead.

"Nope. Boyfriendly duties ended at midnight."

"Are you a pumpkin?"

I laugh, tossing the damp rag into the sink.

"Not a pumpkin, but I don't want to leave you hanging out to dry on your own. Besides, I don't have anything going on today."

"That's a lie," Ollie says, pushing himself to stand.

"What do you mean it's a lie?"

"I know for a fact that you're supposed to be at Naughty Pine."

"Naughty Pine can get by without me for a few hours. Perks of owning the place."

"Are you sure?" Ollie asks.

"Yes, I'm sure." I nod and steer him out toward the living room. "Trust me, if I really needed to be there, I'd be there."

"Have I ever told you what a great friend you are?" Ollie gives me a thankful look as I help him onto the couch and cover him in a blanket.

"Not in the last week." I smile at him.

"You're a really good friend."

"You know I'd do anything for you."

Ollie wraps himself like a burrito in the blanket and starts flipping through the streaming services on his TV while I order us some soup.

This isn't how I planned on spending my Saturday, but it's a pretty good interruption in my usually busy schedule. I order Ollie soup and bread—the blandest I can find to not upset his stomach—and get myself a few more things. I know the bagel isn't going to cut it today.

When I take the spot next to him, Ollie scoots over and burrows in close to me.

"This will make me feel better," he sighs, sinking into me.

"Then I won't go anywhere."

Huh. This is nice.

Ollie and I have always been touchy-feely with each other, but why does this feel different?

I'm tempted to kiss the top of his head. To pull him closer and run my fingers through his hair. But that's not something friends would do.

Boyfriends? Yes.

Friends? No.

The boyfriend clock expired at midnight. I'm back to being Hunter, Ollie's best friend. A title I wear proudly.

I kick my feet out onto the coffee table, and Ollie does the same. I ignore the zing of electricity that shoots through my leg as his toes brush against my calf.

That is definitely *not* a best friend feeling and something I definitely don't need to be experiencing right now.

This is Ollie. He knows everything about me. And I know everything about him.

Well, almost everything.

Because I did just learn the other night that he's still a virgin.

Not that it matters to me, but it has my wheels spinning on who deserves Ollie. He shouldn't give it up to just anyone at this point. No. It needs to be someone who sees him for the special person that he is.

So why does the thought of him dating anybody make me inordinately angry?

"You okay, Hunter?" Ollie asks, peeking one eye up at me.

"Fine, why?"

"You're starting to growl."

"Oh, sorry."

"Is it because the princess is running away and she won't get her Christmas miracle?"

"Yet," I point out, turning my attention back to the movie. "She has to come back to the palace for the miracle to happen."

"These movies are so predictable." Ollie laughs.

"But I still love watching them."

"And it's why you love Celine Dion so much," he chuckles.

"Hey, there's nothing wrong with loving a good power ballad every now and then."

"More like every time you're in the car."

"Hey." I nudge him in his side. "Keep that up and I'll head home."

"Then how will you know if the princess gets her miracle?"

"Yeah, yeah."

One movie turns into two, which turns into three.

Ollie's half asleep in my arms now, half-eaten soup sitting on the coffee table. I don't think I've moved in three hours, but honestly, I can't remember the last time I felt so content.

Usually during the holiday season—from the beginning of November all the way through January—I'm busy. It's hard to take even one minute to myself just to sit down. Being with Ollie like this? I never even gave it a second thought to be honest.

And I love it. Possibly a little too much.

I know he's fast asleep when his hand drops, resting on my thigh.

Crap.

That is a little too close for comfort. I try to shift away, but it just moves with me. Shit. I don't want to think about that hand wrapped around any parts of my body. How good it would feel. How good it would feel to be the one to finally have sex with Ollie.

Ollie. *My best friend.*

God, sex would complicate things way too much. It's the last thing I need to be thinking about. But now that the thoughts are there, they won't go away.

Of peeling him out of his sweater he always wears to work. Of seeing a blush creep up his cheeks. Hell, I wonder if it creeps up anywhere else.

Nope, danger zone.

I do NOT need to be thinking about that.

I need to get out of here before I can act on these feelings. Not when Ollie is tired and vulnerable after last night.

Seeing that darkness has finally started to settle through the windows outside, I extract myself from Ollie's hold.

I lay him down on a pillow and tuck the blanket around him.

"Hunter?" He stirs.

"Sorry. I got called into work."

"Sorry."

I smile down at him. "Nothing to be sorry about."

I pull his glasses off his face and set them on the coffee table. "You rest. I'm sure you'll be feeling a lot better tomorrow."

I turn to leave, but Ollie grabs my hand before I can go.

"Thank you for being here today. And last night."

"Like I said, Ollie,"—I squeeze his hand—"there's nowhere else I'd rather be. Now get some rest and I'll see you tomorrow."

Stepping into my boots, I head outside. A cold bite of wind slaps me in the face and fuck, did I ever need that.

It helps cool every racing thought in my head. Ollie needs to go back in the friend box. Opening that boyfriend box was way too much for me.

Friend zone, friend zone, friend zone.

That's all we'll ever be. And I'll be damn lucky to get to spend my life as his best friend. We're too ingrained into each other's lives to want to risk messing things up by turning this into something else.

Something different.

Sex complicates things. It always does.

Friend zone, friend zone, friend zone.

Now if I keep repeating that to myself, maybe I'll start to believe it.

Chapter Seven

BLAME IT ON ZUMBA

"Hey, Hunter. You've got a customer up front." Brooks pops his head into the office.

"Who is it?"

I shuffle the endless stack of paperwork around on my desk—my least favorite part of my job.

All of it is mind-numbingly dull. I'd rather be out chopping down trees to go to good homes for the holiday season, but having spent Friday night and all day Saturday with Ollie, I'm behind.

"Someone." He smirks.

"Can this someone wait?"

Based on his face, he knows exactly who it is and isn't going to tell me.

The fucker.

"Absolutely not."

The voice that comes around the corner makes my insides clench.

My mother.

Not exactly the person I wanted to show up in my office unannounced. With the amount of work I have to do, this is definitely going to waylay me today.

"Hi, Mom."

I stand, rounding the desk to drop a kiss on her cheek.

"Hi, Mom? That's all you have to say to me? Do you know how many times I've called you this month and nothing? You think you can ignore your mother?" she scolds me. Snowflakes stick to her graying brown hair.

"Mom, I'm not ignoring you. You know it's my busiest time of year. It's not like I can get away whenever I want."

"But you can make time for your *boyfriend?*"

"What? I'm not dating anyone."

"Is that the story you're going with?"

She crosses her arms in front of me. The face she's giving me is eerily similar to mine when I'm questioning things.

Is this what I'm going to look like when I'm her age?

"Yes?" It comes out as more of a question.

She tsks at me. "That's not the story I'm hearing."

"What are you talking about?" The hair on the back of my neck stands on end. I have a feeling I know what she's talking about and I'm not going to like it.

"Oh, just how you were spotted with a *boyfriend* the other night."

"Where are you hearing this from?"

We went to Vanilla Springs. It's where Ollie works. I figured we'd be fine there since it wasn't in Moose Falls.

If people spotted us together in Moose Falls, the gossip train would've left the station before we even got inside.

I lean back against my desk, waiting for my mom's answer.

"I was at Zumba and someone told me how happy you looked with your boyfriend."

"And who told you?"

"Yeah, who told you?" Brooks asks.

"Don't you have somewhere to be?" I ask. I don't need Brooks hearing all of this and running to tell the guys.

"I'm right where I need to be." He grins at me.

The fucker.

"The woman who is the instructor. Her friend's son's girlfriend works at The Hotspot and said she saw you there with a man that you looked quite cozy with."

"Fuck me," I groan.

"Said she heard you call the young man your boyfriend."

This is one of the downsides to small towns and running my business. We're the only Christmas tree farm for at least three towns.

Meaning everyone comes from miles away to get their fresh trees at the Naughty Pine. I know most of the customers, and they recognize me.

Something I didn't even think about when going out with Ollie.

"Well? What do you have to say for yourself?" she asks. "I didn't think you did relationships."

It's not like I can tell my mother it was all a ruse. That would not go over well.

"Look, Mom," I say gently. "We weren't telling anyone because it's new."

"That's what you tell strangers. Not your mother. You tell your mother when you're dating someone."

"Mom." I shove my hand through my hair, pulling at the strands. Maybe it'll help me not be annoyed with her.

"Don't you *Mom* me, Hunter," she says. "I want to meet this young man."

"Mom. That's not taking things slow."

"Bring him by for dinner tonight."

"I have to work."

"Nonsense." She looks at Brooks behind her. "Can you handle things tonight?"

A Cheshire-cat grin is on his face. "Oh, I can absolutely cover so Hunter can take his boyfriend over to meet you."

I subtly flip him off before my mom notices.

"Good." Mom walks over and pecks me on the cheek. "I expect to see you at seven. Do not be late, Hunter."

"It was nice to see you, Mrs. Wells," Brooks calls out as she leaves in a whiff of vanilla-scented perfume.

"You too, dear."

"I really need to get better help," I tell Brooks.

"You love me." He takes his seat and gets back to work.

Ugh. If only he wasn't such a good friend and the best employee I have, I'd fire him. But it's not like he could stop my mother. Hell, she'd convince even the scariest security guard to let her back to my office.

With a tidbit like *I have a boyfriend*, nothing would stop her.

Pulling out my phone, I text Ollie.

HUNTER

I need my boyfriend again

OLLIE

Your boyfriend?

I need you to pretend to be my boyfriend

I thought it was a one-time thing

You don't do boyfriends

Apparently word got around to my mom and she knows I have a boyfriend

So I need you again

Crap

What are we going to do?

Considering we have to be at her house at seven for dinner, I need you to come with me

Are we done after this?

I thought things were going back to normal

Things are always normal

Just playing pretend for a few hours

I don't know what's worse

Me trying to fake it in front of my coworkers

Or fake it in front of your mother

My mom will be okay

She knows you

I've never met her like this before

Yeah, but you've met her

She's the same crazy old lady she's always been

Who now happens to be my boyfriend's mom

Fake boyfriend, Ol

Are you up for this?

I'm cool

Cool, cool, cool, cool, cool

I can do it

Your use of too many cools makes me think otherwise

Nope, I'm good

You helped me

I can help you

What time are you picking me up?

6:45 work?

Get there right at 7

What can I bring?

Nothing

I cannot go empty-handed to meet my boyfriend's mother for the first time

You've already met my mom

It's no big deal

I'm ignoring you on that

I have to impress her

No need to impress

We'll break up quietly after a few weeks and call it a day

Fake boyfriend or not, I'm going to the store

Then I'm not going to talk you out of it

I SMILE, locking my phone to get back to the stack of paperwork I have to finish before another night away from the farm.

We're not even dating and he has to impress my mother. It's just like Ollie. The same feeling I had after his work party bubbles up in me now.

The one where it's nice to have him be *mine*.

Shit. Why does this keep happening to me? I need to push these thoughts aside and focus on the fact that Ollie's my friend.

That's it.

One more night as my fake boyfriend.

Maybe these feelings will be out of my system by tomorrow.

One more night.

That's it.

Chapter Eight

OLLIE

IT WON'T BE HARD

I'm standing outside my front door when Hunter pulls up at the exact time he said he would. I head to his truck, a cold, wet snow starting to fall.

"You brought a poinsettia," Hunter says as I close myself up in the warmth of the truck.

"Sharon went with me to get it. She was way too excited about it," I say.

"I'm sure she was."

"She also said your mother would love a poinsettia."

"She'll appreciate it, even if you didn't need to bring anything."

I roll my eyes at him. "I have to make a good first impression."

"My mom loves you. You have nothing to worry about."

"She loves *friend* Ollie. Not *boyfriend* Ollie."

"Pretty sure they're one and the same." He laughs.

"What are we going to tell your mom?" I ask, ignoring him.

"What do you mean?"

"About how we started dating."

"Stick to the same story we told everyone at your office," he says. "Keep it simple."

"Well, the hard part about that," I start, adjusting my glasses, "is I don't remember a lot of what we told people."

"Because you were drunk off your ass, Ol."

"Hey." I smack him on the arm. "I might still be drunk."

"Well, I made you soup when you were sick and you were so impressed, you had to start dating me."

"Really? Pretty full of yourself there considering I've never tasted your soup."

"What?" he scoffs. "I know I've made you soup."

I turn in my seat, facing him. "Hunter Wells. You have never once in your life made me soup."

"Because I don't know how to make it?"

My jaw drops. "How are we friends?"

Pulling up to the one stoplight in town, he looks over at me, tapping my chin closed. The barest hint of contact has warmth spreading through me. I shouldn't be feeling that.

"You might need to teach me then."

"Really?" I ask. "You want me to show you how to make soup?"

"You teach me how to make soup, and maybe I'll show you how to cut down a tree."

An audible gasp escapes my lips. "Hunter! I have been asking you for years to let me cut down my own tree and you always say I can't."

"Because you told me you can't swing an ax."

"I am going to hold you to this. Next week."

"What are you going to do with the tree?" he asks as we pull into his mom's driveway.

Icicle lights hang from the front porch. Large inflatables fill the yard. A giant snowman. Santa. A Christmas tree. There are even reindeer on the roof.

"I can take it to work," I say, hopping out of the truck.

"Of course you will."

Walking up the sidewalk, my nerves grow.

Damn it. I thought I wouldn't be as worried about this. I mean, it's fake. I shouldn't stress about this. But stressing about things is my baseline. I'm not immune to it.

"Hey." Hunter stops me, grabbing my elbow and giving it a squeeze. "It'll be okay."

The reassuring smile he gives me does funny things to my insides. That doesn't make things easier for me not to worry about this. Now I'm thinking about why my stomach is swooping and swirling at my best friend's smile.

"I know," I say.

My smile wavers, but I take a deep breath as Hunter opens the front door and I follow him inside.

"Mom. We're here."

Sweeping into the living room, his mom is wearing an oversized ugly Christmas sweater covered in snowmen with carrots sticking out from the front. Her grayish-brown hair falls in wavy curls around her shoulders. Her smile lights up her face.

Hunter is the spitting image of her.

"There is my baby boy." She pecks him on the cheek. "And…Ollie?"

"Mom." Hunter rests a hand on my lower back. "You know Ollie, but let me introduce you to him as my boyfriend."

"This is for you, Mrs. Wells." I shove the poinsettia at her in a rush of nerves.

"You're dating Ollie? When did this happen?" She looks from Hunter to me. "And how many times have I told you to call me Karen?"

"I-i-it's new," I stutter.

"I've told you this. It's why we weren't telling people, Mom," he reiterates.

"I'm not people, Hunter. I'm your mother."

She shakes her head as she heads back into the kitchen.

"Are you doing okay?" Hunter asks as he helps me out of my coat.

"Good. Fine. Great. Good."

He smiles down at me. "One too many goods, Ol."

"Sorry."

"Don't be. C'mon, I'll get you a drink and that'll help."

"Not too many though." I point at him, following him into the kitchen.

"Are you going to tell me how this happened?" Karen asks as we push open the door into the kitchen.

"I got sick one time and Hunter brought me soup to make me feel better." I spit it out a little too fast. But my nerves are still getting the best of me.

"My son. What a sweetheart he is. I knew I taught him well. Even if he doesn't return his mother's phone calls."

"Mom," Hunter groans, burying his face in his hands. "I'm busy."

"I'm glad I could peel you away from your trees long enough for dinner," she says.

"You didn't complain when I brought one over for you."

"Which reminds me," she ignores Hunter, "Ollie, since Hunter hasn't been over to hang his ornament, I saved one for you to hang too."

"W-w-what?"

An ornament? That seems like something a *real* boyfriend would do. Damn it. I am his real boyfriend. It's fake to the two of us, but to everyone else? It's the real thing.

"It's fine, dear. Now, can I get you something to drink?"

"I'll have whatever Hunter is having."

"You can have whatever you like," Karen says. "I do have a spiked hot apple cider if you'd like some."

"Actually, that sounds good."

"Just not too much, Ol," Hunter says, nudging me in the elbow.

"Sounds like there is a story there."

Karen pours three glasses of cider and hands one to each of us.

"I had a few too many drinks at my work party. I was a bit nervous for them to meet Hunter."

Her gaze snaps to Hunter's. "His coworkers got to meet Ollie before I met him?"

"Mom, you've known Ollie since we were babies."

"Not as your boyfriend."

"See!" I slap him on the arm. "I told you it's different."

She looks at me. "I swear, I raised him better than this."

Her smile helps put me at ease. *Finally.*

"I don't like you two ganging up on me," Hunter says before taking a gulp of his cider.

She quirks a brow at him as I hold the warm glass between my hands.

"Deal with it, Hunter. I like Ollie and I'm glad you finally found someone."

"He did date a lot," I tell her.

"Excuse me, I am right here," Hunter interjects. "And I didn't date *a lot.*"

Karen beams at me. "He was waiting for you, Ollie."

"I guess I was."

Hunter leans over and kisses my cheek.

Holy shit.

It's something he's done before dozens of times. We've always been affectionate, so why does it feel different now? That same swirly feeling in my gut is coming back.

What in the world? I am not equipped to deal with this. Fake feelings? I can handle those. Real feelings? Those are too murky to want to deal with.

"Ollie, dear?"

"Sorry, what?"

I shake my head, trying to push all the thoughts away. I need to make it through dinner without blowing our cover.

"Do you like Beef Wellington?"

"Oh, yes. Thank you. It smells delicious."

Dinner is easier than I thought it would be. Karen gives Hunter grief over little things like she always does.

Would this be what it would be like if we did this all the time as boyfriends? Is this what I've been missing out on by not having relationships?

My life is good. It will be good after tonight whether Hunter is my boyfriend or not.

Before I know it, we're in the living room hanging our ornaments.

"I saved these two for you," Karen says, passing two over to us.

Hunter hands me one that is cotton balls covered in glitter and he hangs an ax on the tree.

"I think my parents might have this same one at home." I laugh.

I place it on the tree and take in all the different ornaments. Pictures of the two of them at past Christmases.

Hunter with a gap-toothed smile when he was a kid. Crystal baubles. It's a hodgepodge of everything.

I love it.

"I mean, it's the most basic thing I've ever made. Why'd you keep this, Mom?" Hunter asks.

She peeks her head between our shoulders. "I kept every ornament you made. Why wouldn't I?"

"Maybe that's why you decided to open the farm," I say. "You always had a thing for trees."

"Can you have a thing for trees?" He quirks a brow at me.

"Well, if someone were to have a thing for trees, it'd be you," I joke.

"Alright." Hunter rolls his eyes. "Speaking of trees, I have an early morning and need to head home."

"I'm so glad you both came," she says.

"Thank you for having us. Dinner was delicious," I say.

"Ollie, are you going to visit your parents for Christmas?" Karen asks as we slip into our coats.

"I'm staying here this year," I say.

"Then you can come over on Christmas Day."

"What? I don't want to impose." I adjust my glasses, hating that I'm letting my nerves show.

"Nonsense. I don't want you to be alone."

"I—"

"Hunter, I'll text you the details. I'll see you boys soon."

She gives us each a hug before shutting the door behind us.

"So much for one more night," I mutter, shoving my hands in my pockets.

"You can do one more day, Ol," Hunter encourages. "Christmas is two weeks away. No big deal."

"Just until Christmas?"

"Well, at least until after Christmas with my mom."

"Right. Christmas Day."

Hunter opens his truck door for me. "Think you can stand hanging with me until then?"

I roll my eyes. "Please. Like that'll be hard."

It'll only be hard if I can't get my feelings for Hunter under control.

Chapter Nine

OLLIE

SEXY LUMBERJACK DREAMS

He's late. I shouldn't be surprised, but he is.

If there's one thing I know about Hunter, it's that he's not the most punctual of people. Sure, dinner with his mom was one thing. He wouldn't hear the end of it if he were late.

Drinks with our friends? If he's late, none of us care. Especially me. I know he's spent a lot of time away from the Naughty Pine this season, and it's hard for him to be gone during the holidays.

The farm is on the way home from my office, so I offered to pick him up on the way to the bar.

It's what any good boyfriend would do, right?

Giving up on waiting outside in the cold, I walk down the sawdust path to the building that houses the offices.

"Ollie, what are you doing here?" Brooks asks, startled when I come in.

"Hey, Brooks. I told Hunter I'd pick him up for drinks."

"Oh, right." He glances down at his watch. "I lost track of time."

"So did Hunter, apparently."

Brooks shuts his laptop and grabs his coat. "I'll meet you guys over there. I want to see Charlie before the chaos begins."

"Why do you assume it will be chaos?" I ask, stuffing my hands in my pockets.

"Bingo night at the Tinsel Tavern to win free drinks for the night?" A smile stretches across his face. "It's going to be chaos. At least for Griffin and Theo."

"You're probably right. I'll see you over there."

I wave him off, the warm office now quiet. Papers are scattered all over Hunter's desk. It shouldn't surprise me. He's never the most organized of people.

Me? It would drive me crazy to have my desk in a state like this.

Hunter? Never.

Checking my watch again, we're going to be late for the start of the night. I guess it couldn't hurt to go in search of Hunter.

Stepping outside, I see that dusk has fallen. Purples give way to dark blues as the cold settles over Moose Falls.

String lights hang over the sea of trees as far as the eye can see. Happy chatter is heard everywhere.

Turning the corner to start my search, I stop dead in my tracks.

Search over.

Hunter is walking toward me wearing a red plaid shirt stretched tight across his chest with the sleeves rolled up to his elbows, ax in hand. His jeans cling to defined thighs. His light brown hair is perfectly styled, even this late in the day.

Am I drooling at the sight of my best friend?

It feels like I'm drooling. I've seen Hunter like this countless times since we met. It's what he always wears to work.

"Sorry I'm late, Ol," Hunter greets me.

"Late?"

"For Bingo night."

"Oh, r-r-right," I stutter.

I don't know if I'll ever be able to form a coherent sentence again. I've never had sexy lumberjack dreams, but I can see the appeal now. Because I want to climb Hunter like a tree.

Up close, I can see the sweat that sticks to his arms. The small peek of chest hair from the undone buttons on his shirt.

How have I never noticed how sexy Hunter is?

"Ollie?" Hunter asks. "Are you okay?"

A smirk plays on his lips when my gaze snaps up to meet his.

"Umm, yeah."

"You sure? You look flustered."

"Just waiting on you for Bingo." I clear my throat, my voice sounding different than normal in my own head.

Hunter rests a hand on the building behind me. His height overwhelms me. The scent of pine clings to him like a second skin.

I can't help it. I reach up and fist my hands in the soft material of his shirt.

"Now what are you doing?" he asks.

His brown eyes are warm and soft as they gaze down at me.

"I don't know," I confess.

Hunter really should not be walking around like this.

It's doing funny things to me. Things like thinking about what it would be like to kiss him. What it would be like to feel his beard scratch against my jaw.

Against *other* places.

He could have his own sexy lumberjack calendar and I would buy every single copy.

"Do you need help figuring it out?"

Hunter leans closer. His tongue darts out, wetting his lips.

Oh God. Does he want this too? Am I not the only one feeling things here?

Hunter takes another step forward, ax still in one hand. "I…"

Can I make the first move? Do I have it in me?

Before I can do anything, a crash sounds from behind us, causing Hunter to move away from me.

A tray of hot chocolates has dropped and Hunter rushes over to help, taking all of his heat and pine-scented muscles with him.

Damn it.

Sucking down the cold air, I try to steady my thoughts.

Hunter needs to be in the best friend box. Sex and friendship never works out. Well, I'm assuming it wouldn't work out. I'd have to have it to really know.

And I don't want to lose him. He's too important.

I guess it was a good thing that tray of drinks crashed.

No move needs to be made.

Good.

Smoothing my hands down my coat, I walk over to where Hunter is helping clean up.

"Need help?"

He shakes his head. "Almost done. Why don't you wait in the car and I'll be out in a minute?"

"Sounds good."

Because even being that close to Hunter is going to start causing my thoughts to go wild again.

Now I need to figure out how to make it through the rest of the night with him.

Chapter Ten

LOCK IT UP TIGHT

We had a moment.

Ollie, *my best friend*, looked like he wanted to kiss me. His eyes were glowing. Want swirled in his brown irises.

I know what that feeling looks like. What it *feels* like.

Because I was feeling it too.

I wanted nothing more than for Ollie to kiss me, but it didn't happen.

Now, we're sitting across from each other in a crowded bar playing Bingo.

Every now and then, his eyes flit over to me. I know because I've been watching him all night.

I couldn't give a shit about how obvious I'm being.

Because right now, all I want to do is kiss him. Haul him into my lap and taste him. Feel his tongue against mine and wait for the sounds that come from him as I deepen the kiss.

I haven't had this feeling in a long time. Not since I had

my heart broken. I swore off love. So why am I feeling these things with Ollie?

Fuck.

I adjust myself, trying not to draw attention to myself. These are definitely not thoughts I need to be having in a crowded bar.

"You okay?" Griffin elbows me in the side.

"Fine, why?"

"You seem preoccupied."

"Nah, I'm good."

He nods at my empty game cards. "Then why don't you have a single chip down?"

Shit. He's right.

Plastic chips sit in a messy pile next to my cards.

"I don't care if my drinks are free tonight. I can buy my own."

The lie spills from my tongue a little too easily.

"Right." Griffin sips his beer. "Wouldn't have to do with anyone else?"

I sputter over my own drink. "What?"

"B-Seven!" Charlie calls out.

Every table is full tonight, making it harder to hear the numbers. People groan and cheer as he keeps the ball cage moving.

Griffin's gaze moves to Ollie before turning back to me. "You two seem different tonight."

"Why? Because we're not sitting next to each other?"

"And because you won't look at one another." That comment is more on par with what's going on. "Did something happen?"

"Nothing's happened."

Not a lie. But I wanted it to happen. And I think that's part of the problem.

"O-Sixty-Nine!"

Snickers and giggles are heard throughout the bar.

"Real mature, guys. C'mon," Charlie goads.

"Bingo!" Theo yells next to us.

"What? No way!"

"It's too early."

"You can't have it."

"Suck it. I won, losers!" Theo calls out, taking his board up to Charlie to confirm.

"You're a dick, Theo."

He blows a kiss in the direction of whoever said it. "No, but I do like it."

"He is too much sometimes." Griffin shakes his head.

"You got that right."

"I got us all another round." Theo comes back with four drinks in hand. With Charlie manning the Bingo cage, Brooks is helping out behind the bar. "Scooch over."

Sliding across the leather seat of the booth, I'm squished right up against Ollie. Not where I wanted to be, but I don't hate it either.

Because the press of his thigh against mine feels really fucking good.

"Sorry," I whisper as the game starts again.

"It's fine."

He shifts next to me and it does nothing to help the buzzy, floating feeling inside of me.

Who knew the softest touch from my best friend could feel so good?

At least since the guys know this isn't real, we don't have to put on a show. To anyone on the outside looking in, it would look like any other night with our friends.

Which is how I need it to be tonight.

"N-Thirty-one," Charlie calls out.

"How can I be bad at Bingo?" Ollie grumbles next to me, looking over his cards.

"All luck, Ol." I peek over at his cards, and only a few numbers are covered. "I'm not doing much better."

"Because you're not paying attention," Griffin chirps.

He only grins back as I glare at him.

"Maybe if Charlie slowed down, we could get the numbers," Ollie says, squinting at his card.

"Here." I pull open my phone and turn on the flashlight for him.

"That's so much better."

"It's what I'm here for."

Ollie turns to smile at me, looking way happier than anyone should playing Bingo. I want to puff out my chest and beat it like a caveman for doing this small thing for him.

Fuck.

When did I become like this?

Someone who wants to make someone else happy? No, not someone else.

Ollie.

Fuck. Fuck, fuck, fuck.

I was happy. I *am* happy.

My life is good. I shouldn't be worrying about this.

"B-Two," Charlie says into the mic.

"Oh! Bingo! I have Bingo!" Ollie shouts, raising his hand in the air. "I did it."

He leans over and wraps me in a hug.

One that I like a little too much.

"Way to go, Ollie!" Brooks says, coming over with a round of shots for everyone.

"Oh, I don't think I can drink that before driving home."

"I'll drink it." I smile at him and take both shots.

"That means I'm cashing in on my freebie next time," Ollie says around a yawn. "I want a beer and not shots."

Brooks winks at him. "You got it."

"You ready to get out of here?" I ask him, resting my hand on his shoulder.

His gaze tracks the move. "Yes, please."

"C'mon then."

We wave goodbye to the guys as another round starts, dodging between the tables as we leave.

"Thanks for the excuse to get out of there," Ollie says.

"Anytime. I have an early morning to get ready for tomorrow, so figured it was as good of a time as any." I open Ollie's car door. "I'm going to grab a ride share home."

"What? Why? I can drive you."

I shake my head. "It's the opposite direction for you. Go home and get some rest and I'll see you tomorrow, okay?"

"I'll be there. I might need to get toe warmers for my boots if it's going to snow."

A chuckle escapes my lips. "You'll be fine. I promise."

"As long as you keep me warm," Ollie says.

I don't think he realizes what he said, but damn, if I don't want that. To pull him into my arms and let my warmth seep into him.

"I'll see you tomorrow."

"Bye, Hunter."

I stand outside until his brake lights fade into the night.

Shit. I really need to get these feelings under control. I don't have time for a relationship right now. I'm too busy at the farm. Ollie deserves someone who will put him first.

Staying busy tomorrow will help. That and a good night's sleep.

I've got this. I can lock up my feelings for my best friend.

Easy, right?

Chapter Eleven

HUNTER

REAL REAL

Everything looks perfect. Everything is *going* perfect. I don't want to jinx it, but fuck. Everyone is having fun.

The line for hot chocolate and snickerdoodles is longer than the wait for Santa. Happy laughter fills the air as kids take a ride through the trees on the train.

And here comes the person I'm most excited to see.

"Hunter. Wow." The lights sparkle in his eyes. "This looks great."

"Thanks."

"Everyone looks really happy."

"I'm going to take the train out here in a little bit. Want to go for a ride?"

"Sure. I'm going to grab some hot chocolate before." He throws a thumb behind him. "Do you want one?"

I shake my head. "I'm good. Don't go flirting with any other men while you wait."

"Please. Do you think I'm going to go off and find anyone when your mom will be popping up any minute?"

"Just making sure."

He rolls his eyes at me before walking over to take his place in line.

I linger a fraction longer than I should, staring at his ass, before I go help out with taking tickets.

The family fun night is something I started doing a couple of years ago and people love it. Train rides. Santa visiting. Free ornament painting for all the kids.

Everyone loves it—it's one of the best nights of the year. I've always loved working this night.

Tonight? I wish I were walking around with Ollie. Holding his hand, pulling him close.

Shit.

For a fake relationship, I can't stop thinking about Ollie in a very *real* way. Thinking things I haven't felt in a long time. Since I dumped my boyfriend and moved home. I locked all those feelings up. Everyone told me what a grump I was being about relationships. Well, as Charlie said, I was being a dick about relationships.

Maybe it was because I needed someone like Ollie?

Again, not what I need to be thinking about right now. The repetitive task of taking tickets and talking to guests helps clear my thoughts.

"Wow, this place is hopping," Charlie says, walking up hand-in-hand with Brooks.

"Always the most popular night," I say, waving them in.

"Do you want some help?" Brooks ask.

"If you wouldn't mind taking tickets for a bit so I can do one train ride, that'd be great."

"Sure thing. I know you said I didn't have to work, but I can."

"I want you to enjoy your night."

The way I wish I could with Ollie.

Brooks shoves me out of the ticket booth. "Go do some train rides and come back. You can at least have a little fun."

"Thanks."

Kids run by me as I head toward the small platform where the train rides start. Ollie is lingering by the front as kids squeeze into each of the cars.

"You ready to ride?" I smile at him.

"I don't think anyone has ever taken me on a train ride before."

A light snow starts to fall, catching in Ollie's hair. I don't think.

Grasping the back of his neck, I pull him in for a long, slow, sweet kiss. He tastes just like the hot chocolate from the cup in his hands.

"Mmm, delicious," I whisper against his lips.

"Why'd you do that?" he whispers.

"Curious eyes."

"Really?"

"Yeah."

I don't know if anyone is around, but I don't care. Right now, I have to quell this burning need inside of me for Ollie.

It does the opposite. It stokes the fire.

Fuck.

Ollie's eyes are wide behind his glasses as he slides onto the bench seat next to me.

I really shouldn't have done that. Not right before getting into a small space with him. Inhaling the clean soap smell that is Ollie.

"You know, you're concentrating awfully hard on driving this train."

I peek one eye at him. "You know, safety and all."

We come up to the first copse of trees. Inflatables light up the dark night as oohs and aahs come from the back of the train.

"It's a lot more fun up here with you," Ollie says, nudging me in the shoulder.

"Want to learn to be the train conductor?"

"More like I *like* hanging with the conductor as he is now. I would not trust me to drive a train."

I rest my arm along the back. "It's really not hard. It's basically on autopilot at this point."

"Either way. I like being a passenger prince."

"You make a good one." I wink at him.

"Will you let me do this next year too?"

"I promise."

I turn my attention back to the train as we come around to the old barn that's lit up with Christmas lights. The thought of not being with Ollie next year at this time, even though this is fake, shouldn't sting.

"Are you okay, Hunter?" Ollie asks after a few minutes.

"Yeah, I'm fine." My answer is short. Shorter than it usually is.

"You don't seem okay."

"Sorry, just focusing on the train ride."

"Didn't you say this thing could control itself?" He laughs.

"Alright, smart ass," I say to him, trying not to let the thoughts of not being with him get to me.

I know this thing between us is fake, but I don't know, maybe we could…maybe we could get it out of our system? Based on Ollie's reactions to me, I think he might be into it.

But…how do I broach the subject?

The main barn comes into view as I pull into the platform and everyone starts to unload.

What better time than now?

This is my favorite night of the year. Everyone is happy. Painting ornaments. Telling Santa what presents they want.

Before I let Ollie get away, I grab his hand and drag him behind the barn.

"What are we doing?"

Lights shimmer all around us as the heavy smell of pine perfumes the air.

"Can I ask you something?"

"What is it?" Ollie replies.

His cheeks are pink from the cold, his peacoat buttoned all the way up to his neck.

"I don't exactly know how to ask this." I scrub a hand down the back of my neck. Mainly because I don't want to fuck it up because relationships aren't my forte.

"Talk to me, Hunter."

"Well, I know we said this thing would last until Christmas…" I start.

"Right." Ollie fidgets with his glasses.

"Well, what about we made it a real thing until Christmas?"

I worry my bottom lip between my teeth as I watch a flash of emotions cross his face.

"Isn't it supposed to be real?"

"No, I mean, yes. I know it's fake, but what if we just played pretend for now? Like it not be fake, but *real* real."

"I feel like that was a confusing statement."

"Fuck. I am not explaining this well."

"It seems you've turned into a bit of an Ollie."

He smiles up at me.

"Look, I know we're fake dating right now to get through the holidays. But instead of it being fake, let's just, I don't know, be real. Like a real couple."

"You don't like relationships," Ollie points out.

"I like *you.*"

"Does this have anything to do with that kiss earlier?" he asks.

"I mean, it was pretty—"

"Nice," he finishes.

"Only nice?" I fire back.

"I enjoyed it and would not be opposed to more."

Pressing my palm into the side of the barn, I step closer to him. "Is this you agreeing to my plan?"

"Just until Christmas, and then we go back to being friends?"

"We'll always be friends, Ol. Just friends who kiss now."

"I don't think you're kissing me right now," he says.

"Would you like me to change that?"

"Yes. I very much would like you to kiss me again."

I cup Ollie's cold cheek and wrap a hand around his hip to tug him close. I study his face, brushing my thumb over the apple of his cheek. His eyes widen in the low light.

If there's one thing I know about my best friend, it's that I can read him like an open book.

Oh yeah, he definitely wants this.

Leaning down, I suck on his bottom lip. Fuck. He tastes delicious. Even better than before somehow. His soft purrs and whimpers have me moving closer and deepening the angle.

I tease him, nibbling and sucking. I pull back and capture his mouth with mine.

When he gasps, I slide my tongue into his mouth. I can tell he's nervous, but he lets me take control. Something that I gladly do. Light strokes, hard strokes. I know he likes it because he sinks his fingers even harder into the front of my chest. I'm standing impossibly close to him. I push my thigh between his legs and *fuck*. His dick is hard against my jeans.

"Fuck, Ollie." I drop my forehead to his.

"I don't think I've ever had a better kiss in my life," he says. Those lips of his are stung swollen.

"Oh, yeah? I haven't even shown you the good moves."

"The good moves?" His voice is breathless.

I love that I make him feel like this.

"If you think that's good, just you wait."

"What moves are we talking about?"

"More kissing." I press a kiss to the corner of his mouth. "Maybe more." I move my leg between his.

"I-I...I would be amenable to that," he stutters.

"You would be amenable to sex?"

He nods, glassing fogging up.

"Well then, I think tonight has been a very good night."

"Want to make it better?"

"How?" I ask.

"Kiss me."

I smile at him. "I think I'm amenable to that."

Chapter Twelve

OLLIE

WHAT A GOOD BOYFRIEND

Swiping my comb through my hair one last time, I take in my appearance.

Green cable-knit sweater. Dark jeans. I even pulled out a new pair of clear-rimmed glasses for tonight.

It's not the fanciest of outfits, but I like it. I have a feeling that Hunter will too.

Hunter.

A real date with him. My best friend.

I'm nervous and excited.

I want things to go well. He doesn't like relationships. Anytime you bring up a relationship around Hunter, he turns into a growly menace. So when he proposed doing this? I was shocked.

I mean, what if we do this for real and we don't have any chemistry? It would fundamentally change our friendship. I mean, how could I ever look at him again if there's nothing between us?

I can't think about that though. A knock echoes around the house as I give myself one last look in the mirror.

Swinging open the front door, there is Hunter.

And *wow.*

I don't think I've ever seen Hunter look so sexy.

In a denim button-up shirt with a black tie and black slacks, he looks better than I've ever seen him look.

"Hi."

My eyes snap up to Hunter's deep brown ones. A smirk plays on his mouth under that beard of his.

"Hi, Hunter."

"You look nice."

"You look nice too," I parrot back.

An awkward silence fills the space between us. Great. I don't think this is off to the best start.

"Fuck," he groans. "Are you nervous too?"

"Yeah." I nod my head a little too aggressively, my glasses slipping down my nose. "I mean, yes, I am nervous. Very nervous."

Hunter takes my hand and pulls me in close. I collide with his strong chest.

"Want me to help put your nerves at ease?"

"How do you plan on doing that?"

He answers with a kiss. A kiss I feel in every part of my body. His fingers move to the back of my neck, changing the angle.

Hunter overwhelms me in the best way. His scent. His touch. His taste.

"Mmm. I don't know if that had the effect you were wanting."

"No?" His question ghosts my lips.

"I mean, yes on the nerves. But now I want to do more of that."

He gives me a quick peck. "Date first, Ollie. Then we can do much more of that."

Grabbing my coat, Hunter helps me into it as I lock the door on my way out. "Where are we going?"

"I know a cute little place down in Moose Springs."

"Why are we going an hour away when there are perfectly good places in town?"

"Because do you really want everyone in town coming up to us and asking us how our date is going?"

My eyes go wide at the thought. "No."

"I thought so." He swings open his truck door for me. "Maybe next time. Give them something to talk about. Not the first time."

I watch as he jogs around the front of the truck and hops in.

"Can I confess something?" I ask him.

He rests his arm along the back of the seat, the fabric of his shirt stretching with him. I've never noticed these things about Hunter before, but I like that I can now.

"What's that?"

"I already like the thought of a next time."

He kisses me again. "I do too."

Will I ever get used to this feeling of him kissing me? It's good. So good, it's driving me wild. To the point where I want to take him inside and start doing all those things he promised.

It's a quiet drive. Celine's Christmas ballads— and my ever-lusty thoughts, which I keep to myself—carry us to the next town over.

Moose Springs is the exact same as Moose Falls. The same Christmas lights strung over Main Street. Snowbanks plowed to the sides of the roads with kids jumping in and out of them. Storefronts lit up from the inside.

"C'mon. This way."

Hunter takes my hand and leads me down the sidewalk. He doesn't let go as we fall into step next to one another.

"Where are we going?"

A smile catches the corner of his mouth. "How does pizza sound?"

"Pizza? Is that good for a first date?" I ask.

Not that I've been on many, but pizza?

"What do you have against pizza?"

"Nothing."

"We're making our own. I thought it'd be fun."

"Oh. That sounds good."

Hunter grabs me and pushes me up against the side of a brick building. "I know you're picky about what you like to eat, Ol, so I thought this could be fun. If you don't want to, we don't have to."

I shake my head. "No. I like it."

"Good. Because I happen to think it's a great place for a first date."

"Why's that?"

"You'll see."

Hunter leans in like he's going to kiss me, but at the last second, presses a kiss to my cheek and walks off.

"You're mean," I call out behind him, rushing to take his hand again.

"There will be plenty of time for stuff like that. I promise you. There is no way you're leaving tonight without—"

"Without what?" I ask.

His lips ghost my ear. "Without you coming in my mouth."

"Oh."

Oh.

"That's right." Hunter pulls open a fogged-over glass

door and motions me inside with a slap to my ass. "Now, get inside like a good boy so we can make some pizza."

The heavy scents of garlic and tomato greet me, but that's not the only thing. Life-sized cutouts of Celine Dion, Mariah Carey, and Beyoncé line the walls. There's an old Whitney Houston tour poster behind the counter as one of her songs blasts from the speaker.

Laughter burbles out of me. "How in the world did you find this place?"

Hunter's eyes are warm, lighting up his entire face. "You mean this gem? How could I not know about it?"

"Why haven't you brought any of us here before?" I ask, shrugging out of my coat.

"It's my secret." He winks at me.

A younger woman comes by to show us to a table with two balls of dough, various toppings, and a jar of sauce waiting for us.

"Everything is ready for you to start. Make sure you roll out your dough so it's about a quarter of an inch thick so it doesn't burn."

"Thank you," I say before she retreats to another couple walking in.

Aprons sit on each stool. Once I've pulled mine on over my head, Hunter turns his finger in a circle.

"I'll tie it for you."

Strong fingers brush my back.

How have I never felt anything like this before? It's a small, brief touch. Maybe this is why I was never that interested in other guys. They never made me feel like this.

His lips brush against the side of my neck and wow. That felt so damn good.

"There you go." He squeezes my hip.

"Th-thanks," I mutter.

When he takes his side of the table, there's a knowing

look on his face, as he leans across to me. "Ready to make pizza?"

I grab the rolling pin next to me and start in on my hunk of dough. "I don't know if I've ever made pizza before."

"Don't you remember in elementary school? We used to make those mini pizzas for lunch?"

"Oh God." I laugh. "Those were actually terrible. I don't know why anyone let us eat them."

"We're lucky we didn't get food poisoning."

I point at him with my rolling pin, bits of dough falling off. "Speak for yourself. I think I was off school for a week because I got so sick."

Hunter quirks a brow at me. "Well, let's hope that this pizza doesn't make you sick. I'd be awfully sad if I didn't get to spend time with you."

My grin is so wide all my teeth show. "But then you could bring me soup to make me feel better and it's like our dating story is real."

A loud laugh escapes him. "I don't know who brought the other soup at this point, Ol. We're both taking care of each other."

"Good. I'll hold you to that if I need it."

With my dough fully rolled out, I ladle sauce onto it and smooth it around, sneaking glances at Hunter. My eyes roam over his shirt. The way his muscles flex as he works.

I don't know what I want to eat more tonight…Hunter or the pizza.

"How's it going over here?" The woman from earlier pops up, startling me.

"Good," Hunter answers.

"Need any more toppings, or are you okay?"

"I'm good," I say, grabbing a handful of cheese to drop onto my pizza.

"Great. Can I get you anything to drink? Beers, wine? Soda? Water?"

"Two pale ales if you have them."

She smiles. "Coming right up."

"I don't think you have enough cheese there, Ollie," Hunter points out, sauce splattering on the butcher-block table in front of him.

"What?" I look down at my dough, completely hidden under mozzarella. "I like it."

"As long as you left me some."

I toss a piece onto his sauce. "There. I saved that just for you."

He rolls his eyes. "Wow. What a good boyfriend."

"The best."

He reaches over and puts one pepperoni in the middle of mine along with a red pepper. "There. I saved some for you."

He heaps the rest onto his.

"You know that's going to be bad with no cheese on it, right?"

He grabs a handful and mixes it in with the rest of his toppings. "It's going to be delicious."

"Whatever you say."

I take what's left of the pepperoni, sausage, and peppers, placing them in neat circles on top of the cheese. Looking over at Hunter's, his is a discombobulated mess.

It's our friendship in a nutshell. I'm neat and tidy. Hunter is disorganized chaos.

Our drinks are brought out and our pizzas are taken back to be put in the oven.

"All I Want For Christmas" comes on and it's perfect.

"You know, I'm glad you brought me here," I say.

Hunter holds his beer bottle out and I clink mine

against it. "I can't think of anyone else I would want to bring."

"Do they only play music from the people on the walls?"

"Only female singers. It's pretty cool. I'll bring you back for Britney night. You'll love it."

The stupid happy grin on my face is hard to hide, even while taking a sip of my beer.

"That'll be fun."

I don't know why I was so nervous about coming out with Hunter tonight. We've known each other for years. It's not like everything was going to suddenly change. We're still the same people—with the bonus of kissing now.

And later tonight? After pizza?

I can't wait for more.

Chapter Thirteen

OLLIE

FIRST TIMES

An hour is too long.

After scarfing down our pizza in no time flat, we started the long drive home.

I'm antsy. I want Hunter's hands on me. Want everything he told me he'd do to me tonight.

His thumbs are tapping away on his steering wheel as he hums along to the Christmas tune filling the cab.

Must be nice to be so unbothered with what we're about to do.

"What are you thinking about?" he asks, his voice startling me out of my thoughts.

"What? What do you mean?"

"You're staring a hole into the side of my face."

"I'm surprised you noticed."

"Why's that?" A brow quirks in my direction, even in the low light.

"You're just singing along to the radio without a care in the world."

Flipping on his blinker, he pulls off the side of the road and parks the truck.

"Is that what you think?" he asks.

"Umm…"

Now that we're sitting here, I'm not that confident in my answer. Not with the way his eyes are boring into my own.

Swift hands unbuckle my seatbelt and pull me onto his lap. It's a tight fit, but wow. Hunter's hard cock is pressed up against my own quickly hardening one.

His hands sink into my hair as he trails kisses along my jaw.

"Do you think I'm not affected by what we're heading to do? Because it's taking everything in me not to fuck you right here."

"Ergh," I groan.

"Your first time, hell, *our* first time is not going to be smashed together in my truck. I want to take my time with you, Ollie. Peel you out of this sweater and watch you lose control when I put my mouth on you."

I am painfully hard. Harder than I've ever been in my life. Hunter rocks his hips against me. He knows it too.

"Then why are you teasing me?"

Reaching between us, he cups me through my pants. "You have to wait." He sucks on the tender spot on my neck where my pulse is throbbing. Much like my dick. "You deserve a whole lot more than this."

"You shouldn't have pulled over then."

Fisting my hands in his hair, I crash my mouth over his.

It's messy and hot and everything a fiery kiss should be. His beard scratches against my soft jaw as I slide my tongue into his mouth.

I have complete control as I let this kiss consume every

part of me. Every thought as I sweep my tongue into his wet heat.

It feels so damn good, I can't help but rock my hips over him. How easy it would be to come just from this. The vibrations of his moans against my lips fuel me.

Is this what I've been missing out on?

"Shit." I somehow manage to tear my mouth from his as I get way too close to the edge. I do not want to come in my pants after making out with Hunter in the car for the first time.

"You sure you don't want to keep going?" Hunter whispers.

His eyes mirror my own. Hazy, full of lust and desire for the other.

"Like you said." I wiggle myself out of his hold, doing my best not to brush against his erection. "I want you to take your time with me."

"Fuck, Ol. You're driving me crazy."

"Then it's a taste of your own medicine." I slap him on the thigh. "Now get going, because I don't want to wait any longer."

"I really should have picked somewhere closer to home."

He pulls back onto the road, going a bit faster than he was before.

"Next time."

"Next time?" He peeks over at me. "Next time I don't plan on leaving the house with you."

Damn. I certainly hope he's right.

BY THE TIME we pull into my driveway, the tension is

thick. Hunter barely puts the truck in park before I'm hopping out and running to unlock the front door.

I've never been so excited to do anything in my life.

The nerves from earlier tonight are gone. All I want is Hunter.

Who is casually strolling up the front walk like he has all the time in the world. Standing in the doorway, I tap my foot with an air of impatience.

"Why are you taking so long?" I ask, arms crossed as he finally steps into the light of the front porch.

"I can't help it if you look really fucking sexy waiting for me."

I take a step back. "I can go look even sexier naked in my bed."

"Don't you dare." He stops me. "That's my job."

Hunter hefts me into his arms with ease and eats up the space between the front door and my bed in no time.

"I don't think I've ever been carried like this before," I comment.

He sets me down on the edge of my bed and steps between my open legs. "I plan on doing a lot of things tonight you've never done before."

A needy, wanton shudder racks my body as Hunter stares at me.

"What are you going to do f-first?" I ask.

With one hand, Hunter pushes me back on the neatly made bed.

"I am going to get you naked." He grabs the hem of my sweater and tugs it off of me. His hands roam over my chest and stomach, brushing against my nipples. It's like a switch straight to my dick, perking up again after I somehow willed him to stay down on the rest of the trip home.

"This isn't naked, you know."

His hands undo my belt and slowly pull my jeans off of me, tossing them into a pile before removing my socks.

"I'm learning new things about you tonight, Ollie."

"Like what?" I pop up onto my elbows to look at him.

In nothing but my plain, sensible boxer briefs, Hunter's gaze is locked on my dick tenting the soft material.

"How impatient you are."

Instead of removing them, he flattens himself over top of me and kisses me again. My legs wrap around him, grinding into him. My fingers try to find purchase anywhere they can to keep him close.

"Well, I want you to fuck me."

"Not tonight," Hunter says, nibbling on my earlobe.

"Why not?" I whine.

"Because." His lips kiss a warm path down my chest, flicking my nipple. "There will be plenty of time for that. Need to ease into it."

"Next time. I don't need that much time, Hunter," I chastise him. "Can you do something?"

I'm not above begging. I don't care. I want Hunter. I've never wanted anyone or anything in my life as much as I want my best friend in this moment.

He nuzzles his face into my boxer briefs, his mouth closing over the head through the cotton.

I fist my hands into the bed sheets because it feels so damn good.

"I like that I make you feel this good," Hunter says, dragging the waistband of my briefs down, exposing my leaking dick.

"So good," I repeat. "So, so good."

"Mmm." A devilish smile spreads across his face. "Look at how good your cock looks."

He drags a single finger on the vein underneath it.

"It's ready for you."

"Just your dick?"

"M-me too," I say, so amped up that I'm struggling to get my words out.

"I wonder how you taste..." He swipes his thumb through my precum and sucks it into his mouth. "Just like I thought."

"How's that?"

"Fucking delicious."

He crashes his mouth to mine as his hand wraps around my dick, giving it an easy stroke as he smears my leaking cum down it.

He swallows every sound I make as I get closer and closer to tipping over the edge.

"Hunter. I'm really close."

"Hang on."

Standing at the foot of my bed, Hunter disrobes. When he shoves his boxers down, his dick springs out, slapping him in his carved abs.

"Holy shit."

His dick is...well, wow. Not that I have any experience in that department, but if I could dream up the perfect dick? It'd be Hunter's.

"Like what you see?" He gives himself a lazy pull.

"Yes. I can't wait to feel it inside me."

"Something else I've learned. You're a bottom, and will probably be a bossy one at that."

"I can't help it when you look like that," I say.

"Hold on then, Ol. Because you're going to like this."

Dropping to his knees, Hunter pushes my legs apart, sucking one of my balls into his mouth. He lavishes both with attention while working his hand up and down my cock in slow strokes.

"Yes!" I shout.

The way he squeezes and twists his hand? It pulls me

right to the edge, ready to come until he backs off. I want to come, but want this feeling to last.

When he moves his tongue to my rim, I don't know how much more I can take. My balls draw up tight as liquid fire courses through my veins.

It's a pleasure I've never experienced in my life. Only *want* to experience at the hands and mouth of Hunter.

I squeeze my eyes shut, trying to stave off release. "Hunter, I'm going to…I think I'm going to come."

He shifts, pressing his weight down on top of me and taking both of our dicks into his hand. I close my fingers over his as we jack ourselves off to finish.

"Time to come, baby."

The nickname does me in. I'm one giant live wire, sparking as my orgasm slams into me. Ropes of cum explode all over my chest, mixing with Hunter's as he comes on a low growl.

"Hunter. Oh my God."

I keep repeating it over and over again, my breath coming in loud, hard pants. Hunter buries his face in my neck, holding me close.

"Fuck, Ollie."

His hot breath dances across my skin, sending one last wave of cum shooting between us.

"That was…wow."

"Yeah. Really fucking good."

"Only good?" I ask.

"Hey." He kisses my neck. "I said really fucking good."

"Might need to work up to amazing next time."

Hunter brushes his fingers over my cheek. "Trust me. I will make sure it's amazing for you."

I have no doubt he will. Because being with Hunter my first time? It'll be more than I ever could have hoped for.

Chapter Fourteen

HUNTER

LUCKY

"You two seem awfully cozy tonight." Theo has one arm draped along the back of our regular booth, the other picking at the label on his beer bottle.

Ollie snuggles closer into my side, and I press a kiss to the top of his head.

"What can we say? We're enjoying each other's company."

I can hear the happiness in Ollie's voice. Ever since we decided to make this a real thing, the two of us have been trying to spend as much time together as we can. I mean, not that we never did that before, but it seems like every spare second we're spending together.

And I really fucking like it.

I've never had a relationship like this. I've been burned in the past with people not wanting to spend time with me even when we were dating, so between that and my cheating ex, it put me off relationships. Made me hate them, really.

With Ollie though? It's easy. All of it is easy.

"Shouldn't you be cozying up with your boyfriend?" I ask, taking one last sip of my beer.

"Trey's busy tonight," Theo says, annoyance lacing his tone.

"Are we ever going to get to meet him?" Griffin asks. "I find it odd we haven't met him yet."

"We've only been dating a few weeks."

"Is he even real?" Griffin snickers.

"Fuck you." Theo flips him the bird. "Of course he's real. Why wouldn't he be real?"

"He's saying," Charlie interjects before they get going, "we haven't met him and want to. Your friends should approve of the guy you're dating."

"Yeah," Griffin agrees. "We all approve that Hunter is dating Ollie."

"Wait, you don't approve of Ollie dating me?" I question.

"Ollie could do better," Griffin jokes.

"Asshole," I mutter.

"Anyone would be lucky to date Hunter," Ollie says, kissing my cheek.

"Damn straight," I say, looking down at him.

Fuck. I really like how things are going between the two of us right now. They're fun and easy. How they should be when we've put a time limit on this thing.

Something I don't like thinking about. Who would have thought the idea of *not* being in a relationship would be the worst thing? None of my friends would believe it.

"You can see why I wouldn't want to bring Trey around," Theo says, shaking his hand.

"Why not?" Brooks complains.

"Well, you can be a lot."

"Hey!" we all rebut at the same time.

"We are not a lot at all," Charlies says.

"I am absolutely chill all the time," Brooks says.

"Sure you are," Charlie tells him, kissing his cheek.

"I think I might be the most chill person here," Ollie says.

"Are you, though?" Griffin's voice carries through the bar.

"What?" Ollie snaps back. "I totally am, right, Hunter?"

"Umm, sure."

His jaw drops and he's too damn cute.

"See if I let you hang out with me during the blizzard."

"You really wouldn't let me come stay?" I tickle his side, knowing his weakness.

"Stop! That's not fair." He squirms away from me, but I don't let him get far.

"I'd hate to be by myself during the snowstorm of the century."

"They aren't calling it that," he says. "If it were, I'd really make you stay on your own."

"Ouch. I see where I fall."

"Ugh. You two are so cute together. And it's not even real," Theo whines, face concentrating on his drink.

"Right."

Ollie settles back next to me, quiet now.

"At least you have a boyfriend," Griffin says. "I'm not dating anyone."

"Too bad we aren't each other's type," Theo says.

Griffin recoils. "Eww. I do not want to date you."

"Feeling is mutual, believe me," Theo agrees. "Maybe Trey has a friend he can set you up with."

Before Griffin can answer, Charlie hops up. "I'm doing

last call. Anyone want anything else? I want to make sure we all get home before the storm."

"I'm driving us, so I'm good," I say.

"Me too," Ollie confirms.

I shut the farm down early today. The roads won't be great, so I don't want anyone driving in the dark in these conditions if I can help it.

We were busy right up until close. I left everything for another day. I can get caught up later.

The thought of getting to stay curled up at Ollie's house for the next few days? It's the break I didn't know I needed.

"I thought it'd be busier tonight with everyone having to be locked down at home," Brooks comments.

"Everyone's probably already home," Theo says.

Looking around the bar, it's almost dead. A few people are hanging out—locals who live within walking distance —but that's it. Charlie comes back with two drinks in hand and heads back to the bar to start shutting down.

"Are you going over to Trey's?" Ollie asks Theo.

"I think so. Still waiting to hear from him."

"You can always come to my place if he's not free," Griffin tells him.

"No offering your place," I whisper into Ollie's ear.

His expression is confused when he looks up at me.

The plans I have for him? I don't want anyone around. I want to spend the next few days doing nothing but burying myself deep inside this man.

Fuck. That taste of Ollie the other night after our pizza date? It was enough to whet my appetite. It's what's gotten me through these last few days of work. Considering I can't skive off every day, we have to make the most of our time together.

That's exactly what the two of us are going to do. I don't care if the snow never melts.

Because it would mean I'm with Ollie.

And damn, if that isn't the best thing in the world right now.

Chapter Fifteen

A DIRTY DICTIONARY

"Are you almost ready?" I call out.

"One more minute."

Stretching across Ollie's bed, I try to keep my impatience to myself.

After the bar closed, we made a beeline straight to his house. Having everything I need in my overnight bag, there was no stopping.

Like I said, I don't want to waste a minute of my time with Ollie.

I'm ready to start without him when the bathroom door creaks open. Stripped down to nothing but his boxer briefs, he looks sexy as fuck.

"What took so long?" I sit up, holding my hand out to him.

"You know, just needed to get ready."

"Ready?" I ask, tugging him between my legs.

"Just a little nervous. And you know, trying to figure out

a way to tell you I started PReP," he rambles. "I didn't want you to think I was taking this lightly."

"I'm on it too. And have all the supplies." I take a deep breath. "Now, relax."

I press a kiss to his stomach, feeling his body start to relax.

"You have nothing to worry about, Ollie. I'll go as slow as you need, and if you want to stop—"

"No." He cuts me off, sliding his hand through my hair and tugging it so my vision locks with his. "I want this."

"Good. Because I've been dying to have you."

"How do you want me?"

"Do you trust me?" I ask.

He nods. "Implicitly."

"I'm going to make you feel so good, baby. So good."

Pulling his boxers down, I twirl my finger for him to turn around. His plump ass is right there. Ready for me to take.

I nip at it, licking the sting away.

"Mmm."

"You like that?" I do it again on the other side.

"Yes," he whimpers.

Pulling his ass cheeks apart, I dip my tongue between them. Every sound that hits my ears goes straight to my own cock.

I'm already hard as a rock as I bend Ollie over to find the tight pucker of his ass.

"Do you know how much I've wanted to eat you out?" I say, pressing my thumb to the tight hole.

"Do it," he urges me on.

Sucking my thumb into my mouth, I press the tip inside.

"Is that it?" he asks, peering over his shoulder at me.

Swatting his ass, I lick the sting away before devouring

his hole with abandon. Every needy gasp, I swallow down. Every moan, I push my tongue inside him farther as he opens himself up more and more to me.

"God, I'm obsessed with your ass."

"It feels so good, Hunter," he cries.

I pull away, standing and leading him to lie down. His cheeks are pink, eyes hazy with lust.

"It's going to feel even better." Pulling his briefs completely off, I toss them behind me. "Give me your hand."

"Why?"

I smirk as Ollie obeys without thinking, even though he questions me. Holding on to his wrist, I spit into his palm. "I want to watch you jack yourself off."

"And what are you going to do?" he sputters, his eyes hazing over with lust.

I push his ankles up toward his body, opening him up to me. I run a finger over the tight pucker of his ass and watch as he shudders. "I'm going to make sure you're nice and loose before I fuck you."

I don't wait another minute as I lock my eyes onto Ollie's and swipe my tongue down his taint to his ass.

"Holy fuck!" he shouts.

I smile against him as I repeat my movements. His own hand falters, but I reach up to wrap my own around his.

"Keep going."

I'm rocking my own erection into the bed. I do not plan on coming until I'm inside of Ollie.

I love how responsive Ollie is to me. Lavishing him with attention, I lock my eyes on his face, watching every emotion roll over him.

Lust.

Need.

Desire.

Something more that I can't quite put a finger on.

I need to get out of my own head before I do something stupid like tell Ollie how much I love being with him.

Boyfriends don't work out for me. I don't want Ollie to be in the category of failed relationships.

Rocking back onto my heels, I watch as he jacks himself off.

"Ready for more?"

"Yes." He nods, knocking his glasses askew.

Reaching across him, I grab the lube and pour a healthy amount onto my fingers. I warm it up before circling his rim and pushing one thick finger inside.

"Holy shit!" Ollie shouts, voice echoing around the room.

"You like that?" I curl my finger toward me, knowing the minute I find the bundle of nerves that is his prostate.

"Oh my God, I'm going to come."

Leaning over him, I squeeze his hand to slow his moves.

"You are not coming until I am inside of you, do you understand?"

There's a command in my voice that's foreign to even my ears. Damn, if he doesn't bring it out in me.

"That felt so good."

His eyes close as I work my finger in and out of him, stretching him wide before pushing in a second finger to scissor them back and forth.

Ollie's dick is making a mess all over his stomach. I let go of his hand and drag my finger through his cum, bringing it to my lips.

"Look at me."

His gaze snaps open to meet mine as I suck my finger inside my mouth.

"Hunter. Kiss me."

Whatever Ollie wants tonight, he'll get. He pushes up as I lean down to seal my lips against his.

It's hot, delicious, and so fucking good, I might come at the smallest taste of him. Jesus. I've never been so worked up like this with any person before.

Of course I am with Ollie. Being with him means more to me then I'll ever be able to put into words.

"Hunter. Please. Now."

"You sure?" I ask, dropping my forehead to his.

"Yes."

Grabbing a condom, I stand, tossing my own boxers to the side and rolling the rubber over my painfully hard cock. Pouring a healthy amount of lube onto my hand, I spread it out.

"I want you on top," I say, lying down next to him.

"Me?"

I nod. "Yes. That way you can take it as slow as you want."

"O-okay."

"You still good?" I ask, as he sits up next to me.

He nods. "Yeah."

Grasping the back of his neck, I pull him in for a long, slow kiss. Tangling our tongues to get him out of his head.

The first time is always nerve-racking, but I want it to be perfect for him.

"Better?"

"Yeah," he whispers against my lips as he throws one leg over.

Holding my dick, I help him line himself up as I push the tip inside.

Ollie's fingers hold on to my pecs as he pushes down a sliver more.

"Just breathe, and push against me. It helps you relax."

He worries his bottom lip between his teeth as he sinks

down another inch. His breath falters as a flash of pain crosses his face.

"You're big," he says, before I can ask him if he wants to stop.

"Take your time."

"I know."

Grabbing his cock, I slowly stroke him, taking him back to that place of pleasure to move through the pain as he takes more of me. Until I'm fully inside of him.

"You good?"

"I...yeah." I squeeze his dick, urging him to look at me. "It helps that you're doing this with me."

"I wouldn't let anyone else do it," I say.

Once the words escape my lips, I know it's true. No one else deserves Ollie like this. I don't want anyone to see him like this but me.

It hits me like a powerful force, but I know it's true.

I don't want anyone else but Ollie, and I don't want anyone else to have him.

Before I can think more on it, he wiggles his hips, moaning in delight.

"Are you ready?"

"Are you?"

He nods. "Yes."

"Take me. Use me however you want, baby."

Ollie gives his hips a slow roll before pulling up and sliding back down. His body rocks over mine as he finds his rhythm.

One hand jacks him off to keep him in the moment while the other roams over his body. Memorizing every tiny detail that I can.

"Take over, Hunter. I want you to fuck me."

Flipping our positions, I push back inside of Ollie as he locks eyes with me.

Connecting our mouths, my moves are slow and steady as I work myself in and out of him. He readily accepts me. Every time I hit his prostate, he squeezes me closer to him.

"You ready to come?" I whisper against his lips.

"Make me."

Ollie takes my hand and we jack him off until he's coming at my touch.

"Yes! Yes, yes, yes!" he shouts. "Oh my God!"

He's muttering, repeating *yes* and *oh my God* to himself as I keep thrusting inside him. It doesn't take long before my balls draw up tight and I'm erupting inside of him.

"Fuck." I dig my fingers into his sides, holding on as waves of pleasure crash through me. "Fuck. So damn good."

My muscles go limp and I collapse on top of him.

"I need a minute," I breathe against him.

"I'll give you one hundred. I don't think I'm going to be able to move for a week."

"It's a good thing we'll be snowed in then."

"That was…wow."

"How do you feel?" I ask, popping up onto my elbow to look down at him.

"Good."

"Just good?" I smirk.

"Great. Amazing. Whatever other words people use to describe sex." Ollie laughs.

"I'll be sure to grab you a dictionary then."

"That will be one dirty dictionary."

Gathering the strength to pull out, I tie off the condom before grabbing a washcloth to clean him up.

Snow starts to build on the windowsill as I snuggle into bed with Ollie and pull him to my side.

"Thank you."

I brush a lock of hair out of his face. "Why are you thanking me?"

"For making my first time perfect. I'm glad it was you, Hunter."

"Me too."

More than I could ever hope to tell him. For now, the two of us are curled up, with the snow falling and nothing but time on our hands.

Tonight couldn't have been more perfect.

Chapter Sixteen

OLLIE

SNOWED IN

The world is quiet, covered in snow. It's still coming down, the windows frozen over. The road out here still isn't plowed.

It makes it even better.

Curling up into my oversized armchair, I sip my coffee, feeling better than I ever have in my life.

Hunter and I had sex last night. It was perfect. I never imagined my first time would be that good. I should have known that Hunter would make sure it was great.

I'm a little sore, but a good sore. I don't know if it's going to slow us down, because there's still plenty we can do.

"Morning."

Tipping my head backward at the scratchy voice, I see Hunter in a pair of low-slung sweatpants and nothing else. My eyes trail his movement as he pads into the kitchen to pour himself a cup of coffee before dropping onto the sofa.

"Hi."

"How are you feeling?" he asks.

"Great."

"Yeah?" He kicks his feet out, resting them on the side of my chair. "I was worried when I woke up and you weren't there."

I laugh. "That I was going to run out on you in my own house when there looks like a foot of snow outside?"

"Fair point." He snorts.

"Don't worry, Hunter. I woke up early and wanted to come watch the snow fall."

He stares outside, the bright white light shining in his eyes. "It is pretty peaceful."

"You were pretty peaceful too. I didn't want to wake you up."

A smile tugs at the corner of his mouth, even though he doesn't look over at me. "What can I say? I was pretty spent after last night."

"You weren't the only one."

"Think you'd be up for doing more of it?"

This time, Hunter turns a heated gaze toward me. A shudder racks my body. I don't know if I'll ever get used to the way Hunter looks at me.

I was always shy when the guys talked about sex in such a casual way. Maybe it's because I didn't have the right person in my life.

Hunter? He's the only person I'd have felt comfortable doing that with.

"Maybe some fooling around, but I'm a little sore."

"C'mere." He wags his finger at me.

It's like a string is tied from his finger to me because I move immediately, plopping down into his lap.

"Hi," I say again.

Pillow lines crease his cheek. His eyes are still sleepy. In a word? Sexy.

"We have all the time in the world. We're not going anywhere."

"What you're saying is you don't want to have sex today?"

He laughs, putting his coffee mug on the table and wrapping his arms around me.

"Not at all. But what I am saying is we have all day to do nothing. We could watch more Christmas movies. Make hot chocolate. Fool around in the shower if we want. Eat lunch then eat each other." He shrugs a shoulder. "Really, anything we want."

"Anything?"

My thumb traces his mouth. I'm trying to decide where I want to kiss him. Kissing Hunter might be my favorite thing. That flash of want right before our mouths collide and everything slows down and settles around me as we connect in the most visceral of ways.

"If you wanted to have a naked snowball fight, I might have to stop you, but really, anything within reason. I really don't want to freeze my balls off today, Ollie."

"You know, I can't tell you the last time I had a day like this."

"A snow day?"

I nod, taking the last cold sip of coffee and setting my mug next to Hunter's.

"Yes. I mean, when it snows, I'm usually at home by myself. It works for me. I can catch up on projects at work and not feel like I'm getting behind. But for once?"

"For once, it's nice not to have to worry about work," he finishes for me. "I get it."

"I feel like you've been taking a lot of time away from the Naughty Pine."

"Honestly? I wouldn't have done it if I didn't have Brooks. He's been picking up the slack for me."

I smile at him. "I guess it's easy when he lives with Charlie and can see him whenever he wants."

"Are you suggesting we move in together?" He quirks a brow at me. "Because last I checked, I didn't think that was our plan."

"Right." I clear my throat, trying not to let that thought grow claws and sink in. "But I can always come hang out with you while you get some work done."

"Hanging out with you is way better. Everything that needs to be done is getting done. Everyone deserves a break now and then."

"As long as you're not getting in trouble because of it."

Hunter brushes his fingers along my jaw before cupping my cheek. "It's a good thing I'm the boss and can make the rules."

"And what rules are you making now?"

He kisses me. The bitterness of his coffee lingers on his tongue. It's better than any shot of caffeine at waking me up.

"If I want to leave to hang out with you, I can."

"What about the trees?"

"The trees will forgive me. I'll play them some Celine or Mariah and they'll be happy."

"Good. I wouldn't want them to die on us." I laugh.

"I've got good people. Trying to be in a relationship around the holidays is never easy."

"I'll take your word for it."

Hunter grabs the blanket from the back of the couch and wraps it around the two of us. "This is one thing you don't have to take my word for. Falling asleep together on the couch while watching a movie? Pretty damn good."

"Let's do it."

Even though he only woke up a little bit ago, curling up with Hunter under the thick, plush throw is heaven.

Falling asleep in his arms?

It's the only way I want to sleep from now on.

Chapter Seventeen

OLLIE

SOUP BEFORE TREES

Time is moving too fast. Christmas will be here in two days. With the holiday fast approaching, it seems like I've only seen Hunter coming into my house at night and leaving early in the morning.

Which is why I'm heading to the Naughty Pine now. I left work early, insulated cooler in hand, to surprise him. Hunter is a hard worker and deserves someone to take care of him. He's built his business from the ground up, and if I can help him during busy season, I will.

Parking my car, I navigate through the busy rows of people trying to get last-minute trees. Precut options lean against wooden barriers. Pine. Spruce. Evergreen. Hunter has them all.

Waving hi to a few of his workers, I head straight for his office. Brooks isn't here. My guess is he's out helping customers. This close to Christmas, it's all hands on deck.

Setting my cooler down on his desk, I pull out my bowls and utensils, plus the loaf of bread I picked up.

One of Hunter's records spins behind his desk, playing his favorite Christmas music.

Getting everything ready, I pull out my phone and send him a text.

SHEDDING MY COAT, I drape it across Hunter's chair and drop down while waiting for him. It's less than a minute before he's coming inside. Snow sticks to his hat, and a smile peeks out from under his beard. For once, he's wearing a heavy coat.

"This is a nice surprise."

He walks around the desk and gives me a kiss.

"That's a nice way to be greeted," I say.

"What'd you bring me?" He rests his butt against the desk, peering over his shoulder.

"Chicken and rice."

"Smells delicious."

"Eat up. It's cold out there. I don't want you freezing."

He shakes his head, laughing at me as he takes a piece of bread and dunks it into a bowl. "You're the only one that thinks thirty degrees is cold, Ol."

"I am not," I huff. "It's below freezing."

"Trust me, when you're outside cutting down trees when it's two degrees, you like thirty."

I shudder. "No, thank you. I like my office job."

"How's the library planning going?"

"Great. I found a way we can put a slide in around the reading tree for the kids. It'll be great."

"I can't wait to see it once it's all done."

I pull my bowl of soup to me and take a large spoonful. "Don't worry, I'll drag you along once it's finished."

"Do I get to see the 3-D plans once they're done?"

"You know it's not like a computer game with little people moving around."

"It would be cooler." He points his spoon at me before taking another bite.

"That's outside my skillset, Hunter. I don't have a computer design degree."

"Why do I think you could do anything you wanted?"

I stand, stepping between his legs. "Like date you?"

"I was an easy target."

"More like we needed each other." I press a kiss to the tip of his nose.

"I'm glad we did," he confesses. "This has been one of the best holiday seasons I've had in a long time."

"Me too. For once, I'm not sad that I'm missing out on Christmas with my family."

"Even though it means hanging out with me and my mom?"

"It'll make it an even better day."

With the exception of the fact that it's going to be the last time we're together. Though any reasons we can't stay together aren't coming to mind right now.

It was always supposed to be fake, with an easy breakup we tell people about after the holidays, though it turned into something real until Christmas.

Everything with Hunter has been good. So damn good, I don't want to stop.

"Look, I know you're busy. I don't want to keep you."

I put the lid on my soup, no longer hungry, and stick it back in the cooler. I don't need to weigh Hunter down with these wayward thoughts. He's too busy tonight.

"Hey." Hunter stops me before I can leave, helping me into my coat. "Thank you, Ollie. I would have gone all night without more than a handful of cookies."

"I'm glad I can keep you fed."

"Listen, if I can get away, I'm going to try and come over tonight."

"I'll wait up."

"You don't have to."

"I know, but I want to."

Because time is ticking away. If it means staying up a few extra hours to be with Hunter, I'll take it.

Because all the time in the world with him won't be enough.

Chapter Eighteen

NO GOOD DAY

I hate the sinking feeling that settles in my stomach as Ollie and I leave his house. It's Christmas Day. The end of this *real* fake relationship. Ollie needs someone who can give him the time that I can't. And…what if I'm not built to be with someone and screw this whole thing up?

Maybe because it's your best friend?

I push the thought away because that's the one reason I don't want anything to happen to the two of us. These feelings keep washing through me, and they are not fun. Today is supposed to be a fun and joyful day. Not stressing about ending things with Ollie.

With the one person who I might actually love.

Nope, not going to think about that at all.

"You okay over there?" Ollie asks, reaching across the console and resting a warm hand on my forearm.

"Mentally preparing myself for whatever my mom has planned for us today," I say.

"She's not that bad. I like Karen."

"It's because you didn't grow up with her."

"I don't know when you think I magically showed up in your life," Ollie starts, "but I've known your mom as long as I've been alive."

"Yeah, but she's not *your* mom. Big difference. Do you remember how she used to try and embarrass me in high school when I wouldn't say goodbye to her after dropping me off?"

"In her defense, you were too cool for yourself in high school. She was trying to bring you down a peg or two."

"Wow," I say. "The truth comes out."

"You did just fine."

"Please. Only because we were friends."

Even back then, Ollie was my closest friend. I had friends from all different groups, but he was always the one I wanted to do everything with. Ollie was—is—the most important person in my life.

So why am I letting him go at the end of the day?

"We're here."

The drive is so automatic, I don't even realize I'm pulling into my mom's driveway until Ollie is hopping out of the parked truck.

Mom's waiting at the door in a pair of plaid pajamas covered in Christmas trees and a Santa hat on her head.

"Morning, Santa." I snicker, dropping a kiss on her cheek.

"Merry Christmas, boys."

"Merry Christmas, Mom."

"Merry Christmas, Karen. Thanks for inviting me."

"Please. I would never let you spend the day alone now that your parents have gone off to the West Coast." I smile at her, handing off the bag of presents as she reaches for them. "Now, would you like to open gifts first, or do breakfast? I have a pitcher of mimosas ready."

"How about some mimosas and presents?" I ask, toeing off my boots and shrugging out of my coat.

"I like that plan," Ollie agrees, hanging up his coat and scarf.

I toss my jacket on the bench and get the side-eye from my mom. The one that wonders why I can't be more like Ollie.

"I'm surprised Ollie hasn't rubbed off on you more."

I can't answer, because Ollie does for me.

"No matter how long I've known Hunter, that is the one thing he won't change. It's okay—I love him just the way he is."

He presses a kiss to my cheek and follows my mom into the kitchen.

Does he realize what he just said? That he loves me just the way I am?

Fuck. So much for trying to keep a lid on my feelings today. By the time I'm coming into the kitchen, I'm being shooed back into the living room, a drink getting shoved in my hand.

"I have presents for both of you that I want you to open at the same time."

The logs crack with the flames in the fireplace, spreading warmth through the living room. Snow is hanging on after the blizzard last week.

It's the perfect cozy morning.

Sipping on the mimosa, I smile when I realize it's pretty much straight champagne with a splash of orange juice. Just how my mom likes them.

"What'd you get us?" Ollie asks, setting his glass down and taking his box. "I wasn't expecting anything."

She waves him off as he neatly opens his package. "I was not going to let you go home empty-handed. I'm glad these arrived in time. I was worried."

I'm tearing into my package next to Ollie and bark out a laugh at the sight that greets me.

"Oh my God, Mom." I cringe as I pull them out. "I can't believe you did this."

It's a pair of red striped pajamas covered in candy canes and little Ollie faces that have Santa hats on them.

"Look at Ollie's." She claps, her face exuberant.

"These are wonderful, Karen," he says. "I love them."

His are exactly like mine, except they have my face on them.

"You don't have to wear them today, but you could always wear them tonight, or even tomorrow around the house if you want to. But definitely next year, you both have to wear them over."

"Does that mean you're getting us a new set every year?" Ollie asks.

That same sinking feeling in my gut returns. One that swirls with the alcohol now.

Next year we won't be dating. I don't want to look back at this Christmas and think of how much fun this day was only to be back in the friend zone with Ollie.

I don't know if I can handle that.

I suck down half of my mimosa, but it doesn't help quell these raging thoughts. They stay with me as Mom oohs and aahs over the glass planter Ollie got her that changes color in different light. She puts on the new sweater I bought her and does a mini fashion show with it and the new sequined skirt she purchased for New Year's Eve.

If my mom notices a change in my attitude during breakfast, she doesn't say anything. Ollie throws me the occasional look, but I ignore him, chomping on my bacon with a vigorous bite.

"Are you sure I can't send you home with anything

else?" Mom asks Ollie, shoving another full container into his awaiting hands.

"This will feed me for a week. I promise, I'm good. Thank you."

She pecks his cheek before giving me one. "Thank you for bringing Ollie. I had a wonderful time with both of you. It's nice to see you so happy."

"Thanks, Mom. I love you."

"Love you too."

She waves us off as I help Ollie to the truck along the snowy sidewalk. Neither of us is overly talkative on the drive home. He is just as lost in his thoughts as I am.

By the time I'm pulling up to his house, I don't know if I should get out. "Want me to walk you to the door?"

Ollie shakes his head. "I'm okay. Bye, Hunter."

"Bye—"

The door is shut before I can even finish saying anything. My eyes track him going into his house. Shutting the door and turning on the lights.

Fuck.

I don't want to leave. I don't want this thing to end between the two of us.

Why does it have to?

Because I don't do relationships? Well, not since I found my boyfriend cheating on me. What if this is the right one and I screw everything up by letting him go?

Fuck that.

Turning off my truck, I jump out and run to the front door. Except I find a slippery spot and go careening not into solid wood, but straight into Ollie, who had opened the door again.

"Ouch." He whines, rubbing his forehead where our heads smacked together from falling on the floor.

"Are you okay?" I inspect his face, not seeing any damage.

"I think so. Did you forget something?"

"Remember what we said?" I ask.

He gives me a small nod, still rubbing at his head. "Only until Christmas."

"Only Christmas. But, who dumps people right after Christmas? That's just mean."

"So this isn't you coming to dump me then?" Ollie asks.

"No."

"You're going to wait until New Year's then?"

I shake my head. "That would be a terrible way to start a new year. And Valentine's Day is right around the corner. That would be pretty shitty too."

"What you're saying is there is no good day to dump someone?" Hope sparks in his eyes.

"I mean, I don't know of a good day. Do you?" I ask.

"I think they're all terrible when you're in love with someone."

"Do you know you said that earlier?"

"I might have realized it after the fact. But I really couldn't take it back in front of your mom."

"Did you mean it?"

Ollie tips his chin up, brushing his lips against mine. "Yes."

"Good. Because I really fucking love you."

"I love you too. You and me in a real relationship."

"Yeah." I nod. "I really like the sound of that."

"It doesn't make you all growly and grumpy?"

I shake my head. "Fuck, no. Getting to be in love with you, Ollie? Best fucking thing in the world."

Ollie flips us so my back is on the hardwood floor with

his mouth on mine. I don't care that it's uncomfortable. Ollie's warm kisses are worth any amount of pain.

Until a shudder racks his body.

"As much as I love this, Hunter, I'm cold."

"You mean you don't want to make out on the floor in your doorway?"

"Wouldn't having sex in the bedroom be much better?"

"I've turned you into a monster."

He smiles at me. "One that you'll have to deal with forever."

"Damn. What a hardship."

"However will you deal?"

Pulling him up, I sweep Ollie into my arms and kick the door shut.

"I have a feeling I'll find a way."

Epilogue

OLLIE - ELEVEN MONTHS LATER

THE BEST SOUP EVER

"Are you almost done?" I call out.

"I told you, a few more minutes," Hunter says, his back to me. "I'm not the soup-making pro that you are."

"You know I can help you." I stand to head into the kitchen, but it's as if Hunter can sense it and spins.

"No. You sit. This is a special soup just for you."

"Ugh. I'm hungry."

"Trust me, you'll like it." He smirks at me. "Now, let the chef be."

I settle into my kitchen chair, watching Hunter in the kitchen. His T-shirt stretches across his back, his muscles straining against the material. I bite my lip at how sexy he looks right now.

Since he moved in, he fits right into my space. I love it.

I love his boots by the front door. His shelf of vinyl records of his favorite singers in the living room. Getting to wake up to him every morning.

Being with Hunter is better than I ever thought possible. Maybe I was always holding out on a relationship because I was waiting for him.

He's the only person I'll ever be with, and I wouldn't want it any other way.

"Is this a test run for your mom coming over tomorrow for dinner?"

His laugh echoes around. "She knows you're the cook. We don't have to pretend anymore."

"It would make a good gift to make dinner for her."

"I think she'll like the spa more."

"I will say, I like you cooking for me."

"Duly noted, Ollie," Hunter says. "Now, close your eyes."

"Really?" I ask. "It's soup, Hunter."

"Do it." I can hear the laugh in his voice.

"Fine."

I shut my eyes and hear his footsteps pad across the kitchen.

"Okay. Open them."

Hunter is in the seat next to me, the corner of his mouth quirked up into a nervous smile.

I stare down into the soup in front of me, recognition dawning on me.

"Hunter. Do you know what kind of soup this is?"

"I do."

"I think that part is supposed to come later." I smirk.

Hunter grabs my hand. "Well, I thought Marry Me soup was a good way to ask my question to you."

"To marry you?"

Hunter quirks a brow at me. "Are you going to let me ask, or are you going to just assume that's what I'm doing?"

"Well." I adjust my glasses. "When you say you have a

special soup for me and it's Marry Me soup, I think it's a safe assumption."

"Which is why I want to marry you."

"You do?"

He nods. "I do. This whole thing started last Christmas, and my life has been infinitely better since you and I started dating."

"Fake dating." I smile.

"It led us here. To the good parts. To getting to make soup with you. To coming home to you every night. Waking up with you. Going out with the guys. Maybe getting a dog. Doing whatever the hell we want because the two of us can decide whatever we want to do together."

Tears well in my eyes as Hunter continues.

"I want to take you to every work party. Take you to every Christmas at my mom's. Chop down trees with you. Do everything with you."

Taking my hand, Hunter pulls a simple titanium band out of his pocket.

"Ollie Simms, will you marry me?"

The table shakes as I bump into it in my haste to kiss him. I crash my mouth over his as his hands wrap around me in the possessive way I love.

Hunter takes control of the kiss, slowing my moves. His tongue is commanding as it slides into my mouth. The sweet taste of him I love so much drives me wild.

His cock hardens against me as he deepens it. He swallows down my moans as I rock over him.

"Mmm. We need to stop." Hunter pulls back, eyes glazed over.

"Why?"

"Because I made dinner for you."

"And?" I ask.

I'm needy and desperate for Hunter. Soup be damned.

"You're going to need it for energy for what I have planned for us tonight. But…"

"But what?"

Hunter strokes my cheek, looking at me with nothing but love. "You never actually said yes to my question."

"It's a hell yes!"

"Good." He slides the ring on my finger. It's a perfect fit. "That looks pretty damn good there, Ol."

He kisses the metal on my finger.

"I love it." I wiggle my fingers in front of me.

"Will you try my soup? I did work really hard on making it. I had to practice at Brooks and Charlie's place."

"You practiced?" I can't help the goofy grin spreading across my face.

"Yes. I wasn't going to fuck this up."

Pulling the bowl close, I dip my spoon in and blow on the steam. I take a heaping bite, letting the flavors burst on my tongue.

"It's delicious," I tell him, smiling at his eager expression.

"You're not lying?"

"Try it." I hand him the spoon to take his own bite. "You know I'd tell you if it wasn't good."

"Damn. I'd say yes to me on the soup alone."

Linking my fingers behind his neck, I lay one on him. This is one of my favorite things of being with him. Getting to kiss him whenever I want.

"See? Not lying. I might have you make that more often."

He shakes his head. "Only because I proposed to you."

"Then why don't we enjoy it together and then we can head back to the bedroom and really have fun with this proposal?"

"Seriously, sex monster. You are a sex monster, Ollie."

"It's a good thing you didn't include that in your proposal. I can't imagine our parents would like hearing that as part of the story."

"We wouldn't tell anyone that. No one gets to know that but me."

"Just you." I stroke my fingers down his cheek. "I love you, Hunter."

"I love you, Ollie. My life is so much better with you in it."

"You're the best real fiancé ever."

"Eat up so I can show you just how much I love you."

I never knew that when Hunter signed up to be my fake boyfriend that he would be my very real fiancé.

The best decision we ever made.

Want more in Moose Falls? Keep reading for a bonus scene now...

"Trey is cheating on me," Theo cries, sliding into the booth across from me, Ollie, and Hunter.

"What?" I ask. "I thought things were going great for the two of you."

Reaching across the table, Theo grabs the drink sitting in front of Hunter and chugs the rest of it down.

"Do you need a drink?" I ask. "Well, one of your own?"

"God, yes."

At that moment, Charlie walks up to the table and drops down onto the leather seat next to me.

"You okay?" he asks.

"Trey is cheating on me," Theo moans.

"How do you figure that?" Charlie asks.

"Well, he didn't want to come to Ollie and Hunter's engagement party last week, and I thought that was off. And whenever I ask him to go out now, he's always busy," Theo blurts out.

Brooks comes over to the table with a tray of drinks and Theo grabs two, swigging both down.

"What's wrong?" Brooks asks.

"Trey is apparently cheating on him," I say.

"Who doesn't want to spend time with their boyfriend?" Theo groans. "I mean, look at all of you."

He waves a hand around to the couples sitting around the table, all in love.

"How are you going to prove this?" I ask.

"I don't know yet. I need to drink my sorrows away first."

"I'm sorry," Ollie says. "Is there anything we can do?"

He shakes his head. "No. God, I wish I had a relationship like yours."

Ollie and Hunter share a warm look. I know Theo wants a relationship like our friends have, not to be sitting here questioning whether or not his boyfriend is cheating on him.

"Can you talk to him?" Charlie asks. "Maybe it's not what you think it is."

"What else could it be?" Theo casts a glare in his direction. "After a year of dating, why doesn't he want to spend time with me? I mean, that's a giant red flag."

I snort a laugh.

"Griffin," Brooks hisses.

"What? What was that for?" Theo asks.

"It's just…"

Shit. Am I really going to tell Theo that *none* of us like his boyfriend? Forget the fact that none of us have met him, but he never wants to spend time with Theo like he deserves.

"Just what?" he asks again.

"We just don't think Trey is the right person for you," I say, an ounce of trepidation in my voice.

I love Theo. He's my best friend. But the very last thing I want is for him to turn his ire on me.

"The *right* person? He was the *only* person for me."

"There are still plenty of—"

"Don't you dare say fish." Theo points a finger at Ollie, interrupting him. "I don't want another fish. I want Trey."

"Then talk to him," I reiterate.

Theo rolls his eyes at me. "That would not go over well. 'Hey, Trey, are you cheating on me?'"

"This isn't going well," Charlie whispers, for only me to hear.

"I need more drinks. I'm going to the bar," Theo says, stomping off.

"Will you—"

"I've got him," Brooks says, cutting Charlie off and trailing after him.

"Okay, do we really think Trey is cheating on him?" I ask, leaning across the table.

"Oh, he totally is," Charlie agrees. "I've never liked the guy."

"We've never met him," I clarify.

"And that says something," Hunter says. "If he hasn't met Theo's friends, there's a problem."

"I'm glad we were already friends," Ollie says, love-filled eyes turned to Hunter.

"Me too."

He pecks him, and sometimes, being around people so loved up makes it hard to be single. I'm not looking. I'm happy with where my life is. I really am.

But other times? Like right now? It would be nice to have someone.

These moments are few and far between.

"What should we do?" Ollie asks. "Encourage him to find out, or let it be?"

"I'm really going to regret this, but should we do it ourselves? Find out if Trey is cheating on Theo?"

"Would you?"

Shit.

Theo chose the wrong moment to come back to the table. If only I'd double-checked before saying it.

"Uhh…"

Theo drops down across from me and grabs my hands in his. "Please, Griff? I wouldn't ask if it weren't important."

"Wait, why me? Why not the other guys?"

"You suggested it," Hunter not-so-helpfully points out.

"Fine."

I fight the groan.

"Oh my God. You're the best, Griff. Really. If he's not cheating, then I know he really loves me and we should move in together," Theo says.

"Maybe you might need to have a discussion with him before that," Brooks says. "You're making some big leaps here."

"That's a great idea," I agree. "You can't go from he's cheating on me to moving in with him in the blink of an eye."

"Let's see if he is cheating," Ollie says. "Don't go jumping to conclusions."

"You're right. He's not cheating." Theo takes a healthy swallow of his drink. "I don't know why I'm so worried."

I won't point out that he is worried because that wouldn't be helpful at this point. Ollie looks like he wants to say it too, but Hunter stops him before he can.

"Send me his address," I say.

"You got it." Theo taps on his phone, my own buzzing in my pocket. "Trey is at kickboxing tonight and has to work tomorrow night."

"Wait." My hand stalls, not taking a sip of my drink. "You want me to do it tonight?"

Theo shrugs a shoulder. "Or tomorrow night. I mean, the sooner the better, right?"

I swallow the entire contents of my drink. "Okay, fine. But you can't pester me all night."

"I won't. I promise."

"Really?" I look over at him. He's going to bug me until I do it.

"I mean, I'll at least try," he says.

"You owe me several drinks for doing this," I say.

"Oh, your entire bar tab will be paid."

Brooks snorts. "Considering most of you drink for free, I'll believe it when I see it."

"I really need to start charging them," Charlie tells him.

"Hey, it's all you, not me," Brooks defends.

"Yeah, yeah."

"Okay, if I'm going to see if Trey is cheating on Theo, I need to get going." I knock back the rest of my drink and stand.

"You're the best," Theo says. "Really. If I ever say you're not, remind me of this moment."

"I will." I wink at him. Grabbing my coat, I slide into it and zip it up. "If anything happens, you're paying my bail."

I only hope it doesn't come to that…

Also by Emily Silver

Moose Falls, Maine

Merry in Moose Falls

A Grump in Moose Falls

Want more LGBTQIA+ romance? Check these out:

A French Fling

Off The Deep End

Sideline Infraction

Power Pose

Best of Both Worlds

Love Pucked

For a complete list of all my books, please visit my website.

For a breakdown of my books by trope, check out my trope guide now.

About the Author

Image by Tricia B @TheSmutFairy

After winning a Young Author's Award in second grade, Emily Silver was destined to be a writer. She loves writing inclusive stories, with strong heroines and the swoony men who fall for them.

A lover of all things romance, Emily started writing books set in her favorite places around the world. As an avid traveler, she's been to all seven continents and sailed around the globe.

When she's not writing, Emily can be found sipping cocktails on her porch, reading all the romance she can get her hands on and planning her next big adventure!

Find her on social media to stay up to date on all her adventures and upcoming releases!

www.ingramcontent.com/pod-product-compliance
Lightning Source LLC
Chambersburg PA
CBHW031410310726

48971CB00003B/810